SUNDOWN AMBUSH

Sheriff Dan Slayter leaned against the corral and looked across the meadow. There had been just enough daylight left to find the few cigarette butts and empty cartridge casings that he had put in a bag for evidence. Now there was only a streak of red left in the western sky as night came to the valley.

Something caught his eye on the ground by his feet, and as he leaned over a rifle sounded and a bullet slammed into a corral post where his chest had been.

Dan grabbed his rifle, levered a bullet into the chamber and peered into the darkness looking for flashes of light from a rifle barrel. But the shooting had stopped. Now there was just the whisper of the evening wind and the realization that someone looking to carve a notch on his gun was waiting in the dark evening shadows.

BEST OF THE WEST
from Zebra Books

THOMPSON'S MOUNTAIN   (2042, $3.95)
by G. Clifton Wisler

Jeff Thompson was a boy of fifteen when his pa refused to sell out his mountain to the Union Pacific and got gunned down in return, along with the boy's mother. Jeff fled to Colorado, but he knew he'd even the score with the railroad man who had his parents killed . . . and either death or glory was at the end of the vengeance trail he'd blaze!

BROTHER WOLF   (1728, $2.95)
by Dan Parkinson

Only two men could help Lattimer run down the sheriff's killers—a stranger named Stillwell and an Apache who was as deadly with a Colt as he was with a knife. One of them would see justice done—from the muzzle of a six-gun.

BLOOD ARROW   (1549, $2.50)
by Dan Parkinson
Randall Kerry returned to his camp to find his companion slaughtered and scalped. With a war cry as wild as the savages,' the young scout raced forward with his pistol held high to meet them in battle.

THUNDERLAND   (1991, $3.50)
by Dan Parkinson

Men were suddenly dying all around Jonathan, and he needed to know why—before he became the next bloody victim of the ancient sword that would shape the future of the Texas frontier.

Available wherever paperbacks are sold, or order direct from the Publisher. Send cover price plus 50¢ per copy for mailing and handling to Zebra Books, Dept. 2413, 475 Park Avenue South, New York, N.Y. 10016. Residents of New York, New Jersey and Pennsylvania must include sales tax. DO NOT SEND CASH.

MOUNTAIN SHERIFF

#3 THE CANYON MOUNTAIN WAR
EARL MURRAY

ZEBRA BOOKS
KENSINGTON PUBLISHING CORP.

Chapter One

From the front porch of the ranch house, Martha Green watched while her husband rode into the corrals from the pasture at the base of the mountain. She knew by instinct that he was angry and that he had discovered something up on Canyon Mountain that demanded urgent attention. She only hoped that he wouldn't take his rifle up there again.

Martha was middle-aged, with bands of gray through hair once nearly black. Her blue eyes were young but her face had become lined over the years with worry and concern. This morning those lines cut deeper into her face as she realized her husband was planning something that would bring bad trouble to them.

She ran out to the corrals, where her husband was dismounting. The family dog, Bigalow, was running alongside her, yapping and whining. Bigalow was an old Blue Heeler who had been the family dog for years. Now even the dog could sense the urgency.

Martha reached the corrals and looked through

the poles at her husband. He was standing with his hands on his hips, looking back up the mountain.

"What did you find up there, Jack?" she asked.

"Just what I expected," he answered. "Cut fences. Tracks all over the place, especially near the corral. Big Jed Barlow and his Cross Twelve hands are getting ready to move against us. Unless I miss my guess, they'll be going up there in the next couple of nights."

"We don't have to let them have our stock," Martha said. "Put the bulls in another pasture."

He turned to her. "What other pasture, Martha? There's no grass left down here below. I have to put them back up there. That's the only place left where there's decent grass and water. I have no choice."

Martha took a deep breath. She now looked up toward the mountain herself. At her feet, Bigalow whined and paced back and forth with his ears erect.

"Did my rifle come back from Utah yet?" Jack asked.

"Jack, I know what you're thinking," she said. "Don't do it. Call the sheriff if you have to, but don't go back up there alone."

"We can't stand to lose any more cattle," he told her. "I'm sick of it. Now, I asked you — did the rifle get here yet?"

Martha knew she couldn't lie to him. He had sent his .30-06 rifle down to a friend in Salt Lake City for modification. One of the best — if not *the* best — firearms expert in the country worked out of a little gun and black powder shop in the southern part of Salt Lake City. Just after he had gone up onto the mountain, the UPS man had delivered the rifle — now a semi-automatic equipped to take large clips.

"The rifle came," Martha finally said. "Dear Lord, I wish you would come to your senses."

"Do you want to lose this ranch?" he asked.

"Then call the sheriff," Martha said again. "If you have evidence of rustling, call the sheriff. He'll come out. You know him."

"There are a lot of tracks up there, Martha. But that doesn't prove anything. Big Jed Barlow is careful about leaving evidence."

"Jack, you can't fight them alone," Martha said.

"I've got to do something," Jack said. "And soon."

Jack Green was tall and redheaded and stood his ground, just as his father had before him. The Green Ranch had been established in the valley for over a hundred years. The Green family had a tradition of sticking with it through thick and thin — and holding onto what was theirs no matter what happened.

Besides the normal worries of drought and grasshoppers, the Green Ranch was being squeezed on its north boundary. While Jack was growing up he could remember the continual harassment from their neighbors, the Cross 12 Ranch. The Barlows had been in the valley as long as the Greens, and there was no love lost between the two families.

7

Jack had heard the story often from his grandfather, and then from his father—the shootout on the Fourth of July down in Clark City. It had happened in 1889, a fight over the outcome of a horse race that had culminated in the death of two Green brothers and two Barlow brothers. And another Green brother had died at the funeral, bushwhacked by a Barlow hired hand. The hand had stood trial and was then hanged, but the Barlow family was satisfied: there was one less of the Green family to contend with.

The feud had lasted through the years, with fights and occasional shooting back and forth. The sides had been even up until four years ago, when Jack Green lost his sole remaining brother to a car accident. That left Jack and his family alone to fight the Cross 12 Ranch.

Big Jed Barlow had a younger brother Jack Green's age helping him run the Cross 12. Chet Barlow was every bit as insolent as his older brother and he had a particular dislike for Jack Green. When his older brother, Jed, wasn't stealing cattle or cutting fences, Chet was. Between the two of them, they were picking the Green Ranch clean.

The main reason for the added aggression by the Barlows was Canyon Mountain. Jack Green had bought another piece of rangeland up on the mountain, deeply angering the Barlows. They had wanted the Canyon Mountain pasture badly but had been trying to swindle the owner. Jack Green had stepped in and paid good money to improve

8

his spread. Now Big Jed Barlow wanted to make him pay.

"Did you take the gun out of the box?" Jack asked Martha.

Martha shook her head. "Why would I want to do that? Why would I want to see the weapon that's going to cost me my husband's life."

"If we don't have this ranch," Jack Green said, "then I might as well not have a life."

Martha watched while her husband walked past her and toward the house. Bigalow stayed behind with her and whined. She thought about going into the house and talking to him some more about changing his mind. She knew when he had sent the gun to Utah that he meant to fight the Barlows, to the last man.

She then leaned back against a corral post and clutched at her chest. The pain was acting up again. The doctor had told her to take it easy and not let things upset her so much. Her metabolism rate was like that of a woman much younger than her and when she became nervous or excited, her heart didn't get enough oxygen to function properly.

As a result, Martha suffered chest pains on a regular basis. The lack of oxygen would result in a lower pulse rate and she would feel as if she were going to experience a heart attack. On occasions she had been forced to lie down in bed for periods of hours to allow her heart rate to go back up. She had been into the hospital more than once to be placed on oxygen. But that got to be expensive.

9

Now she was wondering what she was going to do if she became weak once more and her heart began to hurt. She knew she had better get back into the house and lie down. She tried to make herself relax and gather enough strength to begin the walk back from the corrals.

Jack came back from the house with the rifle. He noticed her leaning against the corrals and knew immediately what the problem was. He laid the rifle against a post and started to help her into the house. But she pushed him away.

"Martha, you're letting yourself get excited again," he said.

"What do you expect?" she said, her voice hoarse with pain and anger. "I have to stand here while you contemplate getting yourself killed and you wonder why my heart acts up. Don't try to help me. I can manage myself."

"Martha, you've got to stop worrying. You heard what the doctor said."

"And so did you. It seems to me you are doing a lot to cause this problem of mine. Jack, can't you understand why I worry constantly."

"Martha, I have to go after the Barlows if we're going to keep the ranch," he said. "They intend to steal our last two Charolais bulls and break us if possible. Then they want to take over this place. You know that."

"This is something for the sheriff," Martha said again. "If you will get Dan Slayter up there, he can get things straightened out without a lot of bloodshed. It's been going on too long. Besides, Lucy will be home from college in a couple of weeks. And she wants to bring that rodeo rider she's been seeing. I don't want them coming home to trouble."

"Big Jed Barlow doesn't care who's coming home and who isn't," Jack said. "He wants this ranch, plain and simple. I don't intend to let him have it."

"Have it your way then," Martha said. She turned in anger and made her way back toward the house, holding her chest. Bigalow stood whining, looking first at Jack and then to Martha. He finally turned and loped toward the house to join Martha.

When Martha got into the house, she leaned against the kitchen table. Her hands were shaking. Bigalow was at the door whining and she yelled out to the old dog to be quiet and lie down. She went to the picture window in the living room and looked out.

She saw Jack looking back up toward Canyon Mountain again. The rifle was still resting against the post. He picked it up and looked back up at the mountain, then set it back down again. Then Martha watched him take the saddle and bridle off the horse. Tears of relief formed in her eyes and she took a deep breath. She had talked him out of it — but for how long?

Dan Slayter walked over to his desk and picked up the phone. As sheriff of River County he had gotten to know most of the landowners as well as the businessmen and a great number of the people in town. But there were some of the ranchers who kept to themselves quite a bit and didn't mingle much with others. Jack Green and his wife, Martha, were like that.

· So it surprised him when he heard the woman on the other end of the line introduce herself as Martha Green, and then tell him she had been meaning to talk to him for a long time about a family problem. She wanted to meet him in town, at a little cafe known as the Yallerstone Eatery.

As the youngest sheriff in the history of River County, or in the history of Montana for that matter, Dan Slayter was known as a rebel who had chosen the positive side of the law. He was tall and dark and walked with the confidence brought with being raised in the mountains. Raised as an orphan by his grandfather, Dan had learned the ways of the land early. His great grandmother had been a Blackfoot Indian, so Dan had come to know the ways of the mountains easily and now the land was deep within him.

Dan Slayter was just starting his third year in office and the citizens had come to know and respect him greatly. He was the type of man who could look anyone in the eye, rich or poor, and treat them equally. He was afraid of no one and anyone who broke the law in his county was assured they would not be able to get away from him, no matter where they tried to hide out.

Dan had solved a lot of cases in the back country and he was used to going places after outlaws where nothing else seemed to work. It wasn't uncommon for him to go deep into the mountains to find criminals who evaded every other method of search techniques.

Everyone in the county knew that the Cross 12 Ranch operated for the most part outside the law. But Big Jed Barlow was always very careful not to overdo things. He committed his crimes in patterns hard to trace so that he could erase evidence and be around when the time came to steal more cattle or horses, or somehow make a deal to take over a ranch.

Dan knew from what Martha Green was saying over the phone that she wanted to talk about her husband and their problems with the Cross 12 Ranch. He hung up the phone and went to the desk of his deputy, Leon Walters. Leon had worked with him ever since he had been elected to office. Leon's experience in law enforcement in Alabama had prepared him for the difficulties of keeping the peace in the mountains of southwestern Montana.

"I think this feud between the Barlows and the Greens is coming to a head again," Dan said to Leon. "I'm going to meet with Martha Green downtown. If something comes up real fast, I may need to have you ready to move with me on a moment's notice."

"What about those lost hikers down by Gardiner?" Leon asked. "It sounds like we're going to have to go up and look for them."

"Let's play that by ear," Dan said. "There are a lot of people out looking for them already, including Park rangers. If they don't get results by tonight, we may have to help. But I'm afraid this thing between the Barlows and the Greens is going to erupt at any time."

Leon nodded. "I'll be ready when you call."

Dan left the office with the feeling that the hikers lost above Gardiner were in need of help and that there would be people who could come to their aid before something drastic happened. In the case of Jack and Martha Green, he wasn't so sure. It seemed to him that Big Jed Barlow was intent on having the Green Ranch for himself and that he would stop at nothing to get it.

Chapter Two

Dan was in the Yallerstone Eatery waiting when Martha came in. She wore jeans and a loose-fitting cotton shirt, with a lot of makeup to cover the heavy wrinkles she had developed over the years. Dan couldn't help thinking she had worried half of her life away—either over her husband, or her daughter, Lucy.

It was easy to see that Martha Green had never been totally happy in her life. Her heart problem affected her emotionally as well as physically and the continuous trouble with Big Jed Barlow and the Cross 12 Ranch was rapidly wearing her down. She was now at a point of desperation.

"I don't know how to begin this," she said, after ordering coffee. "I guess the best thing is to just spit it out."

Dan nodded. "That would be best."

"I'm worried about my husband, Jack," she said. "We've been having problems with the new pasture up on Canyon Mountain. Big Jed Barlow is cutting our fences. I'm afraid Jack is going to do something foolish."

"Has he told you this?" Dan asked.

"He sent a big game rifle down to a specialist in Salt Lake City. The rifle came back reworked to kill men, not deer."

"I take it you've tried to stop him and he won't listen."

Martha nodded. "He won't listen to me at all. He says he can't let the Barlows ruin us. He feels the Cross Twelve is going to make a move against our Canyon Mountain pasture very soon. If that happens, we could lose the ranch."

"Why didn't you bring your husband in with you?" Dan asked.

"Because he doesn't believe in asking for help," Martha answered. "He's so headstrong it's ridiculous. I'm just afraid it's going to cost him his life."

Dan thought about what Martha had said. His hunch that the friction between the Green Ranch and the Cross 12 Ranch was getting serious was certainly proving out. Whatever problems the two families had had in the past occurred before his time in office. But there wasn't anybody in River County who didn't know about the Green-Barlow feud.

There were any number of stories about the ongoing feud between the two families over the years, and how they had torn up the Bar and Grill on three separate occasions. There were court records that went way back concerning disturbing the peace cases filed against both families. Dan was certain there were a lot of fights and confrontations that had never been reported. He wondered how many on both sides had been killed and no one had stood trial for murder.

But the two families were now narrowed down to just Jack Green and the two Barlow brothers, Big Jed and his brother, Chet. It would seem the two factions would want to put an end to it all before both families were gone. But now it seemed that the feud was starting up again.

"I just know that Jack isn't going to stop until he's gotten rid of both Barlows," Martha said. "I've heard him say more than once that he won't sleep sound until the skunks are out from under the barn. And I know he means it."

"He should have come in with you," Dan said. "We can handle this thing without all the bloodshed. He's got to understand that he can't take the law into his own hands."

"He doesn't feel the law is on his side," Martha said. "And to be truthful with you, I can understand his thinking. Big Jed Barlow has gotten away with an awful lot over the years. He does as he pleases."

"Why don't you tell your husband that I will be out first thing in the morning and we can ride up onto the mountain and look at those fences," Dan said. "I can make some imprints of bootprints and look for other evidence. If something is going on, I'll put a stop to it."

"I sure hope you can," Martha said to him. "Our daughter, Lucy, is graduating from college in a couple of weeks and she wants to come back home to visit. She is seeing a rodeo rider and they plan to eventually marry. His name is Ben Hutton. Do you know him?"

Dan nodded. "Yes, I know him. I met him on a pack trip into the mountains some years ago."

Dan didn't know Ben Hutton real well, but certainly well enough to know that he was likely looking to get into a family he thought had money. Ben Hutton worked the rodeo circuit, but never got into the big money. Dan had met him during a pack trip into the Bob Marshall Wilderness in northern Montana. Dan had been hired to take a team of photographers from the East Coast in to get pictures of the Chinese Wall and Scapegoat Mountain area. It had been an unusual trip.

Ben Hutton had been a wrangler at the guest ranch where the photographers were staying. Ben was not used to how photographers work and the long amounts of time they take in setting up their scenic photographs. He became impatient a number of times and commented that the light conditions were not going to make the pictures any better. He said often though that he would like to have his name mentioned in the book as the official horse wrangler on the trip.

Though Dan didn't know Lucy Green at all, he was sure that she was somehow fascinated by Ben Hutton's stories rather than what he actually accomplished. But it didn't sound quite reasonable to Dan to think that Jack and Martha Green's daughter would be taken by somebody who wasn't genuine. He decided he would not pass any judgments, though. Perhaps Ben Hutton had changed; but he didn't think so.

"I hope all this can be cleared up before your daughter and Ben Hutton come to visit," Dan said.

Martha looked at him and her eyes were filled with gratitude. She reached across the table and put one of her hands on his.

"I really do appreciate this, Sheriff Slayter," she said. "I know you're a busy man. I really do thank you."

"I would rather prevent a problem than have to go out after something has already happened," Dan said. "Tell him I'll be out first thing in the morning."

Martha Green left the cafe smiling. Dan watched her climb into a pickup parked along the street and drive away. He finished his coffee and walked out to his Jeep, wondering how he might put a stop to the bitterness between the Greens and the Barlows. Though he hadn't yet witnessed any of it, a number of Dan's friends had told him that it was only a matter of time until the lid came off again. Dan just hoped the lid stayed on until the following morning.

Big Jed Barlow burped and got up from the table. His large frame dwarfed the young waiter beside him, who stepped aside and presented him with a cigar. Barlow chose the one he wanted, then bit off the end and spit it out onto the floor. Then he told the waiter to pick it up and throw it away.

Barlow had just consumed two twelve ounce

steaks and three baked potatoes, plus a full six-pack of beer. He wiped his mouth once more with the sleeve of his shirt as he dismissed the waiter, a young man dressed in an 1880's porter-style suit. Barlow liked to pretend he was a cattle baron from the early days of the West and kept his house and its furnishings in the tradition of the last century.

Big Jed Barlow had money and he could afford the expensive antiques that were scattered everywhere in the huge ranch house where he lived with his younger brother, Chet. After their father's death, they had been given the ranch to run as they saw fit. The two of them had shared the house ever since the death of their mother, and since neither of them had ever cared to marry, there was plenty of room.

The Barlows were known throughout the valley as a family who got what they wanted. The local women stayed clear of the two and Big Jed Barlow always said they weren't of his caliber anyway. Every weekend he would send one of the hired hands to the Bozeman Airport in one of the ranch's many vehicles to pick up girls flown in from Las Vegas or Phoenix or San Diego, or whatever city he might choose at the time. No one ever asked him about how he made his decisions.

Though Big Jed Barlow was large and always dressed in dark, ragged clothes, it was his face which scared people. A ring had once caught his lower lip during a barroom brawl, leaving it split to the bone at a cross-angle. Barlow had never bothered to have it sewed up and it had healed with a large V notch in the lip.

That same brawl, or another one, had produced another scar along the side of his nose just under his left eye, crossing downward to where it trailed off over his upper lip. There were those who maintained that both scars were made by the same man with the same ring, a man who later died from a gunshot wound while hunting. They had found him with the top of his head missing, the apparent victim of a hunting accident.

The scars made Big Jed Barlow's dark features seem that much darker. The scar on his face made people think he might be shedding tears of dark scar tissue, and the jagged mark in his lip made him appear as if he was slightly grinning all the time. And it exposed a gold tooth that Barlow always worked with his tongue, as if cleaning it.

But Jed Barlow didn't care about his appearance or what people thought of his looks. The Cross 12 Ranch had brought a good deal of money to the family over the years. The Barlows could buy and sell almost everyone in the valley—everyone but Jack Green.

And Jack Green was on Big Jed Barlow's mind this evening as he worked on the cigar the waiter had given him. He stood at the window with three of his top hands and his younger brother, Chet. Outside, the sun had fallen and the sky was streaked with layers of crimson. They were all looking out at Canyon Mountain.

"Do you figure that helicopter will make it tonight?" Chet asked Big Jed.

"It had damn well better," was Jed's answer. "Jack Green just turned that big bull up into his new pasture. This would be the night to get it out and take it north across the border." He laughed and blew smoke from the cigar. "Just think, a couple of bulls worth fifty grand apiece—here today, gone tomorrow. Jack Green will have to sell out then." He laughed again.

Chet Barlow and the three hands laughed with Big Jed. It was Chet who did most of the planning, though Jed did all the ordering around. Chet wasn't nearly as big as his older brother. He was dark complected, like most all the Barlows, but he was smaller in stature. He was a lot smaller than the average Barlow male and he took a lot of harassment about it from Big Jed.

"We had better hope that Jack Green doesn't get a hunch and ride up on Canyon Mountain to watch over those bulls," Chet said. "That could mean trouble."

"You afraid of Jack Green?" Jed asked.

Chet grunted. "That's not the point. It just wouldn't be a good idea if he showed up, is all. Then we'd have to kill him. How would we explain that?"

Big Jed shrugged. "Why explain it?"

Everyone laughed but Chet.

"I'm serious," Chet said. "I know Jack Green is going to be watching that pasture, especially since we cut the fences. I'm just thinking we ought to wait a couple of days before we go up after the bull—just a couple of days to let Green settle down."

"We haven't got a couple of days," Big Jed told his brother. "That helicopter comes in from Canada tonight. We've got this chance, so we'll take it."

Chet Barlow knew he wasn't about to get anywhere with his older brother. They had been planning this rustling trip for a number of weeks now. They knew that Jack Green had put the bulls up in the Canyon Mountain pasture early because of the shortage of grass. They also knew he would be turning his cows in up there very soon as well. But they wanted to get the two bulls quickly, so that there would be pressure to either buy new bulls—which he couldn't possibly afford—or pay a fee to a neighbor to have their bulls inseminate his cattle.

Jack Green would be forced to sell out eventually then. Big Jed Barlow knew he could continue to steal cows after the bulls were gone and still make a good profit. The plan which had always worked before was to drug the bulls with an injection shot from a tranquilizer rifle and then tie big ropes around them. They would each in turn then be hauled to a big semi-truck waiting nearby. Then they would be hauled into the mountains of the Flathead River country and their brands changed. From there they would be taken into Canada and sold. A simple process that would break Jack Green.

"It will all work just fine," Big Jed told Chet. "You just relax and we'll make sure you're happy. How's that?"

Chet grunted. "You make it sound pretty simple. I'm not so sure about all of this."

Then one of the hands who had been eating at the table with them spoke up. He was small and light complected and considered by Big Jed to be the top hand. His name was Brice Foster and he was an expert at fixing brands and stealing livestock. Foster used a running iron with the skill of an old-time thief. He could change almost any brand there was into something else.

"Relax, Chet," Foster said. "It will all be over before you know it."

Chet resented Foster's tone of voice. Ever since Foster had arrived, it was as if he had become the brother to Big Jed Barlow and Chet had been reduced to a hired hand.

"I wasn't talking to you," Chet told Foster. "You weren't hired to make the decisions around here. You do just what you're told. So no more interruptions."

Foster smirked and threw up his hands as if Chet were holding a gun on him. "Okay, okay. Just trying to make things easier is all."

Big Jed had hired Foster especially for the purpose of taking over the Green Ranch. Foster had already changed the brands on a number of Jack Green's purebred Charolais cattle and it had proved very profitable to the Cross 12. Foster was part of the plan to get the two Charolais bulls captured, re-branded, and sold up in Canada. Foster had had a lot of experience doing that kind of thing.

And Foster had a way of conning people. Chet could see how well Foster was doing with Big Jed. That was why Foster got away with so much now. He could eat in the main house any time he wanted and he could pick from the women Big Jed brought in on the weekend before any of the other hands. As if those privileges weren't enough, Chet was well aware that Big Jed was paying Foster a great deal more in wages than he was any of the other hands, plus he was going to give Foster a percentage of what the take on the bulls turned out to be. And now it looked like he was trying to work his way into having a say on how the ranch was run.

Chet looked at Big Jed and wondered if there wasn't some way he could make his brother see that he was making a mistake with Foster.

"What if Foster doesn't come through with all he's supposed to do in this?" Chet asked Big Jed. "What if he screws up and we're left holding the bag, just waiting for the law to come down on us?"

"I've never screwed up," Foster told Chet angrily. "Not once. Why in hell would you say that?"

"There's always a first time," Chet said. "And your first time could be tonight."

"Bullshit!" Foster spat. "You're just trying to get to me. That's all."

"It's working," Chet said.

"Bullshit!" Foster yelled louder this time. "Nothing's going to go wrong."

Chet just nodded. "Right. I hear you, Foster. Right."

"Have you got everything you need to put those bulls down so we can load them up?" Big Jed asked Foster.

Foster nodded. He reached into his pocket and pulled out a small plastic vial. He was still glaring at Chet, who was smiling himself now.

"This will put them both in dreamland for a good long time," Foster said.

"Just don't kill them," Big Jed warned. "Those bulls are worth a lot of money."

"Have I killed any of the others?" Foster asked.

"I have to agree with Chet, there's always a first time," Big Jed told him.

"What happens if he does kill those bulls?" Chet then asked his brother again. "Nobody answered my question the first time. What happens? Does he pay for it?"

Big Jed ignored the question again and started for the gun cabinet. Chet scowled as he watched Big Jed unlock the cabinet and pick out a rifle. Foster and other hands stood by while Big Jed handed them each a rifle as well. Then Big Jed noticed Chet standing around watching. Big Jed took the cigar from his mouth and snorted.

"You coming?"

Chet finally nodded and came forward for a rifle. Then, as the sound of a helicopter came into the ranch house from outside, he followed Big Jed and the hands out the door.

Chapter Three

The house was still, but Jack Green's mind was thrashing. He lay in bed looking at the black ceiling while he drove himself to a decision. All he could think about was the modified .30-06 rifle that rested in his gun cabinet. He knew instinctively this would the night when the Barlows would try to take his new bull from the Canyon Mountain pasture. It was time to put an end to it or lose the ranch.

Martha had told him that Dan Slayter was coming out when the sun rose, but Jack felt he couldn't wait for Slayter. The Barlows were making their move now, at this very instant, and there wasn't a minute to waste.

Starlight poured in the open window and a summer breeze rustled the thin curtains as Jack slipped out of bed. He left Martha sleeping soundly. He could not tell her he was going; she wouldn't understand. She had told him in detail about her meeting with Sheriff Dan Slayter in town and how he had warned against doing things on their own. But Jack Green was tired of letting Big Jed Barlow have his way.

Jack reasoned that if he went up on Canyon Mountain and caught Big Jed Barlow in the act, he and his hands might back down and leave. Jack was sure it was a helicopter they had been using to move the bulls and stock cows out of the pasture. But he needed to see it happening to help Dan Slayter put Barlow behind bars.

Martha was still sleeping soundly, confident everything would be fine until morning when Slayter arrived. Jack took his clothes into the living room and dressed, then moved to the gun cabinet and selected the modified .30-06. He had tried the rifle out that evening and found it shot accurately. He didn't think Barlow would push things; but if Barlow wanted a fight, Jack felt confident that the .30-06 would help him stand his ground.

Jack turned the knob on the front door slowly and eased out into the night. Bigalow got up from his bed and began to whine. Jack told him to be quiet and go back to bed. As Jack went from the house to the barn, he worked a plan through his mind. He would go up the back side of the mountain and catch Barlow and the Cross 12 hands when they didn't expect him. Then he would have his satisfaction and nearly a hundred years of feuding would come to an end.

He saddled his horse, confident that by the time Dan Slayter arrived he would have enough evidence against Big Jed Barlow to keep him off Green Ranch property forever.

Jack turned his horse up the trail that led out

from the ranch to the back side of Canyon Mountain. The ranch was located at the base of the mountain on Bullis Creek and the trail wound up the property line to an open meadow near the top of the mountain. He reasoned that by this time Barlow and his hands would already be up there and actively working to find his prize Charolais bulls.

The Green Ranch had once owned four of those Charolais bulls, valued at over fifty thousand dollars apiece. But now they were down to just the two, and they couldn't afford to lose either the bulls or any more stock cows.

The ride to the top of the mountain seemed peaceful enough. Jack Green wondered at the vast sky of stars and shining planets that filled the huge black open with dots of light. The moon was high overhead, nearly full and a milky white. It would have been a beautiful night to enjoy had it not been for the rifle he balanced across his saddle.

Near the top the trail skirted a high rock cliff that reached across the southern face of the mountain. It was steep and treacherous here, the only place where Jack worried about the horse's footing. And riding along the cliff at night was dangerous in itself, as the light of the moon was not strong enough to shine clear down below to the base of jagged rocks and deadfall timber.

Jack breathed a sigh of relief as his horse crossed the last stretch of trail along the cliff. He checked his rifle to be sure it was ready to fire. In just a matter of moments he would be coming up over the top into the meadow, and he would be giving Big Jed Barlow and the Cross 12 hands the surprise of their life.

As Jack rode up and looked across the meadow, he saw things just as he had imagined them. A number of horses were tied to the poles of his corral and there were men standing around in a circle a way out from the corral. Jack surmised they were looking down at one of his prize Charolais bulls, already being prepared for shipment out.

And the means of shipping the bull, the expensive but effective method Barlow used to move the stock without taking them off the mountain, was parked near the middle of the meadow. The moon shone off the blades and sides of a helicopter and even as Jack looked at it, he heard the engine start up and saw the blades begin to turn.

Seething with anger, Jack charged out into the meadow. In a matter of moments Barlow and the others would have the bull tied up in the ropes and then secured to the helicopter. Jack knew he didn't have any time to lose.

As he urged his horse forward into a run, Jack noticed the helicopter rising into the air. He saw Barlow and his men scattering in every direction across the meadow. His Charolais bull lay still in the grass, partially secured by ropes. There was a man on his knees over the bull and he was the last one to rise and try to run.

Jack Green stopped his horse and started firing the rifle. Each time he pulled the trigger the rifle would send a bullet toward the running man. Finally, Jack saw the man turn a half-circle and fall into the grass. Jack got ready to aim again when, from behind him, he heard the sound of a rifle.

The bullet whizzed over Jack's head and he pulled his horse up as he saw Barlow and his men taking positions in different parts of the meadow. Some of them had reached their horses and were coming at him already. In addition, the helicopter was headed straight for him as well.

Jack's horse went into an immediate panic and turned to run away from the helicopter. Jack dropped the rifle and grabbed the saddle horn to keep from falling off. There was no way to control the horse now and it squealed in terror as the helicopter roared and turned up just above Jack, just missing the trees.

The horse took him down off the top and onto the trail that led down the mountain. There was a lot of yelling from behind now, as Jed Barlow and his men closed in. The rifle fire continued, sending bullets whizzing past Jack Green's head and body. He pulled back as hard as he could on the reins, as the horse was going way too fast for the narrow trail along the mountainside. But there was no stopping the crazed horse and Jack knew he had no choice but to ride this one out.

As he fought to stay on the horse, Jack once again heard the helicopter coming toward him. He cursed and tried to hold his horse back. They were nearing the trail along the cliff. But the horse was blinded by terror and as the helicopter closed in, the horse surged even faster.

The cliff was just in front of them when the helicopter roared past them just overhead. Jack heard the horse squeal again and felt it jerk to one side, and then stumble. There was no stopping them and the sliding horse took Jack Green off the edge of the cliff and far down into the rocks below.

The magpies were at the bedroom window early, chattering and scolding from the apple tree near the corner of the house. They usually waited at the barn for Jack to throw them table scraps from breakfast. But this morning they knew for some reason that he wasn't coming out to the barn.

Martha awakened to the chattering and sat up in bed. The bedroom window was open and a magpie was sitting on the sill watching her. Behind the magpie was the pink-scarlet light of a new day. Suddenly the magpie flew away and Martha turned to the empty spot in the bed beside her.

"Jack?" she called. "Jack, are you in the kitchen?" She waited awhile. "Jack, where are you?"

There was no answer and Martha got out of bed. She didn't even bother to find a robe as she scurried into the living room. Her stomach began to churn as she saw the door to the gun cabinet ajar. She wanted to scream; it was plain that Jack hadn't waited for Dan Slayter to arrive.

Martha ran out of the house and looked toward

the barn. Just outside on the porch was Bigalow. The old dog was whining. Bigalow was always with Jack, Martha knew, and if he had left the Blue Heeler home, he had gone someplace dangerous.

Martha felt her stomach turning into knots. She ran off the porch and out into the yard to look toward the barn. Maybe he hadn't left yet. She called for him, but got no answer. Bigalow continued to whine.

She ran to the barn with Bigalow at her heels. She stopped when she saw that her husband's saddle was missing from the nail just inside the door.

"Oh, God no!" she said to herself. She shook her head. Out beyond the barn, at the edge of the trail that led up on Canyon Mountain, Bigalow stood looking up the trail with his ears erect. He wanted her to follow him.

Without hesitating, Martha turned and went back to the house and got dressed. When she was finished the sun was just cutting the edge of the mountain tops to the east. She thought about waiting for Dan Slayter; but if Jack was hurt in some way, he might need immediate help. She left a note on the front door saying where she had gone and why. Then, with Bigalow watching, she saddled a horse and rode up the trail toward the top of Canyon Mountain.

She rode with her head swimming, calling out to Jack at regular intervals. Despite the knowledge within her that Jack had come up for one purpose and one purpose only, she held out some hope that he was up on top and just checking cattle, and that he was fine. But she knew better—she knew he had gone after Big Jed Barlow and that he had likely found him.

The mountain seemed to take forever to climb. She urged her horse onward, struggling to keep her panic down within her. She finally got to the point that she became indifferent, working herself to the point of realizing she might not find her husband alive and that she would have to deal with it.

The thought had no more than left her mind when she heard Bigalow whining somewhere down off the trail below. Martha was working her horse along the high cliff that faced the southern side of the mountain. Her mind was up on top.

Martha stopped her horse and listened again to hear Bigalow's barking. She got down from the saddle and tied the horse to a nearby tree, then edged down the slope to look over. Lying still on the rocks below was Jack's horse. Just a bit away was Bigalow, whining and licking Jack's dead face.

Martha caught herself to keep from collapsing and falling over the cliff herself. She pulled herself back up onto the trail to her horse, the vision on the rocks below vivid in her mind. She sat down heavily on the trail and covered her face with her hands. The tears ran in streams down her face and she shook with sobs. Big Jed Barlow had finally gotten the last of the Green brothers.

Dan stood at the base of the cliff with the

county coroner discussing what might have possibly caused the fall and death of Jack Green. Dan was wondering why a man would ride up onto a mountain in the middle of the night and end up in a heap, with nothing to show how it had happened.

The coroner was shrugging. "I don't know where you will begin investigating this," he said. "Something strange must have happened here, but there's not much evidence to go on."

While deputies took pictures of the scene and Dan stared at Jack Green's body, the coroner took more notes.

"Maybe the autopsy will show something," he said. "I know it doesn't make sense, but maybe it was just an accident."

"There's more to it than that," Dan said. "I'm going back up on top and work with the deputies looking for evidence."

Dan rode the treacherous trail across the top of the cliff and came out into the meadow. There he found Leon working with two other deputies to try and understand what had happened the night before.

"There's all kinds of horse tracks up here," Leon said. "And tracks from that bull. But now there's no bull up here and nothing to go on. All we've got is empty cartridge shells and that won't help much."

"How about the helicopter tracks?" Dan asked. "have you found anyplace else where it might have set down?"

"Just the one location, near where the bull was lying," Leon said.

"Have you found any pieces of clothing or anything like that?" Dan asked.

Leon shook his head. "I tell you, there's nothing here."

"Let's look awhile longer," Dan said. "Then we'll call it quits."

Dan worked his way around the corrals, inside and out, while Leon and the other deputies spread out once more and covered ground they had been over at least twice before. Each of them looked as hard as they had previously. One of them had a metal detector and found another cartridge shell. Then Dan found something that made him sure there had been a shootout the night before.

"Look at this," Dan said to Leon and the other deputies. He reached down into the base of a heavy clump of grass and with his handkerchief, pulled up a small plastic tube covered with blood.

"What is it?" Leon asked. "A vial for some drug?"

Dan nodded. "I'll bet we can get some fingerprints off this."

Dan had seen vials like that many times before when he had been working in wildlife biology. The small plastic vials were filled with a drug that would put animals asleep. The vial was attached to a syringe through which the drug was transported into the animal's bloodstream. In this case Dan knew the vial had been used to sedate the bull before transporting it away by helicopter. But he was puzzled by the blood all over it.

"Do you think that the bull bled a lot when they stuck him with the needle?" Leon asked.

"I really doubt it," Dan said. He was looking the vial over closely. "There is a lot of blood on one side, more than on the other. That means the vial was lying somewhere when the blood was spilled on it. We'll have to send it to the lab and see if it's animal or maybe human."

"It's a good thing you came up here," Leon said with a laugh. "We might've looked all day and never seen that. But I doubt if it's Jack Green's blood."

"I don't think it is, either," Dan agreed. "But I want to know whose blood it is. Somehow or another I've got to prove that Jack Green didn't just die in an accident."

They looked around for a while longer and Dan found a small blotch of blood on one of the grass plants a short way from where he had picked up the vial. He took this sample of blood as well and placed the grass with the blood on it into another plastic bag. It seemed certain in Dan's mind that someone had been shot up on top before Jack Green had gone over the cliff.

Now it was seeming more and more obvious that Jack Green had somehow been forced over the cliff. Most likely a helicopter Big Jed Barlow and his hands had been using was buzzing Jack Green and his horse. But there was no way to prove it and no way to call Big Jed Barlow a murderer.

But the blood was most likely human and Dan

knew if he could somehow connect the finger-prints and the blood samples on the vial with someone from the Cross 12, there might be the beginning of a case against Barlow.

Dan left Leon in charge and climbed onto his horse. The search and rescue team would take over and bring the body down the mountain. Martha Green was alone at her house, now terribly empty since being robbed of her husband. Dan intended to stop in and see if he couldn't talk her into going into town and staying at least until her daughter arrived. But that wouldn't be easy, as Martha Green never wanted to leave the ranch for any length of time, for any reason.

As Dan rode down the mountain, he wondered what was to become of the Green Ranch. It was going to be hard now for Martha to hang onto the ranch, with the last of the prize bulls gone and little capital to invest back into the herd. It seemed impossible to imagine that she could run the operation all by herself. Her husband had worked day and night to keep everything going and Martha had been right beside him all the time, going into the house only to fix meals and take care of domestic chores. Now she was going to have to do all of it alone—a task no one would envy.

Chapter Four

At the bottom of Canyon Mountain was the Green Ranch. Dan rode into the corral and watered his horse before he removed the saddle. He wondered if Martha's daughter would want to come back to the ranch now that her father was dead, or if she would want to just go somewhere else and forget about it.

He had no way of knowing how close Lucy Green had been to her father or if there was any real attachment to the ranch. He had never met Lucy Green, but somehow he felt she would decide to come out and help her mother. He had heard Martha talk about her enough at the Yallerstone Eatery to feel that he did know her. It seemed that she wouldn't allow the death of her father to stop her from keeping the ranch together. And when she got over the hurt and pain of losing her father, she would certainly be mad about it.

The fact that Lucy was seeing Ben Hutton interested Dan to a great degree. Since talking with

Martha Green in the Yallerstone Eatery, Dan had learned that Ben Hutton was now working part-time as a stock inspector—during the time when he was not on the rodeo circuit.

Dan kept thinking that Ben was surely going to get mixed up in this affair with the Cross 12 one way or another. And that wouldn't necessarily be good, whether he was a stock inspector or not. From the pack trip into the Bob Marshall Wilderness, Dan knew Ben would want to handle things his own way and impress Lucy and her mother. Even though Ben Hutton was intelligent and knew what he wanted, he was prone to acting on impulse. Ben wasn't one to sort things out before he made decisions. He acted first and let the chips fall where they may.

Dan realized that the chances were good that Ben Hutton would be looking into the feud between the Greens and the Barlows with a keen eye, hoping to help Lucy in any way he could. If he could keep the Green Ranch out of Big Jed Barlow's grasp, he would surely have Lucy Green's hand for the asking—plus a ranch of his very own to run.

But all that wasn't what needed immediate attention. Jack Green's death overshadowed everything else at this time. Now Dan just wanted to let Martha know that he was going to do his best to find out what had happened. He could see no evidence that Jack had been pushed over the cliff, though it did occur to him that hazing by a helicopter could have spooked the horse bad enough to bolt ahead blindly through the dark.

He wasn't sure if he wanted to discuss that with Martha or not. In the short time he had known Martha Green, he had learned that she was nearly as impulsive as her husband. But she went from one extreme to another and wasn't impulsive all the time, like her husband had been. Still, Dan didn't want to say anything that might provoke her into something she would later regret.

Dan went from the barn to the house and knocked on the door. Martha's welcome was in a stronger voice than Dan had anticipated. He found her in the living room gazing out the picture window toward Canyon Mountain. Somewhere high along the trail the search and rescue team was bringing down the body of her husband.

"I sure am sorry about all this," Dan said. "If there is anything I can do for you, please let me know what it is."

Martha Green turned slowly from the window. Her brown eyes seemed expressionless, but there was something in them that told Dan she had come to a decision. She looked up at him and brushed a lock of hair from in front of her face. Her cheeks were dry now, her tears flushed totally from her system. Now she seemed angry and determined to a degree — feeling within herself that she was now going to have to take up where her husband left off.

"I don't know how to tell you this, Sheriff," she said in a low tone. "My husband died to save this ranch. The Cross Twelve Ranch is responsible. So I may have to kill Big Jed Barlow now myself to keep what's mine. What do you think of that?"

Dan looked into her stern face for a moment before he answered. There was something within Martha Green that told him she was determined to make things work for her on this ranch and that she wasn't going to stop until the death of her husband was avenged.

"Are you totally sure the Barlows are responsible for this?" Dan asked.

"Without a shadow of a doubt," Martha Green answered. "I would stake my last thin dime on it. And in fact I am doing just that."

"What do you mean?"

"I mean that I intend to make this ranch stay afloat no matter what it takes. If it takes day and night and every last coin of money I have, I'm going to keep this place alive. And I'm not going to let Big Jed Barlow have it."

Dan nodded. "If you can give me any information that will help you, I would be glad to pursue it. But without facts, I can't accuse Barlow of anything."

"I'll tell you some facts," Martha said. "In the last two years we have lost three prize Charolais bulls valued at over fifty thousand dollars apiece. There is no question that Big Jed Barlow and the Cross Twelve Ranch has been behind it."

"Do you have any idea where the bulls might have been taken?" Dan asked. "There seems little question that they were lifted off the mountain by helicopter. But they must have been taken by the helicopter to where they could be transported either out of state or out of the country—possibly to Canada."

"All we know is they just vanished," Martha said. "Neither Jack nor I ever did know where they went. But I'll tell you something, that isn't going to continue."

"I understand you've lost a number of beef cattle as well," Dan said. "Why didn't Jack report this? Why didn't he get a stock detective in here?"

"Jack was a proud man," Martha said. "Proud and stubborn. He didn't want anybody else fighting his battles. His family has been butting heads with the Barlows ever since this country opened up. None of the Greens ever asked for help from anybody. They just stood their ground and fought toe-to-toe."

"The Cross Twelve is a big spread," Dan said. "Barlow has been grabbing land from everybody around him. Somehow he manages to get it down on legal paper sooner or later. One man can't fight those odds—not and win."

Martha turned and looked out the window again. She bit her lip and clutched her dress in her fists. After a moment she took a deep breath. She knew she had to keep herself under control. Otherwise her heart would act up and she could end up losing her life. But she wasn't going to give up what her husband had fought and given his life for.

In addition, Martha Green had also become very attached to the land that the Green Ranch owned. There were any number of places near the ranch that gave her comfort and happiness. She looked out the window once again and turned back to Dan.

"You see that old pine tree up there at the edge of the mountain?" she asked him. "There is one standing all by itself. Do you see it?"

"I see it," Dan answered.

"Lucy, our daughter, used to climb that tree when she was small. Any number of times Jack had to go out and climb up into that tree to bring her down. I've watched that tree get bigger as Lucy grew up and went off to school. I've told that tree a lot of my problems over the years. I don't intend to go away and leave that tree for Big Jed Barlow."

Dan turned his hat in his hands. "I understand," he said. "I told you I would help you any way I could. I mean that."

"I know you mean it," she said. "But Jed Barlow is so slick in how he operates. He has a way of getting around the law somehow."

"He can only do it for so long," Dan pointed out. "Sooner or later he'll make a mistake."

"I hope so," Martha said. "I really hope so. Because if he doesn't go to jail before long, I'm going over to the Cross Twelve and put a bullet in his head."

"It wouldn't be worth it, Martha," Dan said. "You would only find yourself suffering a great deal."

She turned again to him. "Well, it couldn't be a whole hell of a lot worse than it is right now."

"Maybe not," Dan said. "But at least now you've got that tree to talk to. In jail you've got only bars and walls."

"Whose side are you on?" Martha asked.

"Justice," Dan said. "I know it's hard to think that justice is always carried out, but you've got to believe that in this county it's going to prevail. If Big Jed Barlow is behind your husband's death, I will bring him in sooner or later. You can count on that."

"Just do it before Lucy gets her dander up," Martha said. "I'm going to have to call her at college and she's going to be upset. She's a lot like her father."

"I can understand," Dan said. "I'm looking into things right now and I intend to make sure I know just what happened on that mountain last night. But you've got to realize that putting things together just doesn't happen overnight."

"Yes, I know," Martha said. "But Jed Barlow is responsible either directly or indirectly for the death of my husband. And one way or another, he's going to pay. I promise you, Sheriff Dan Slayter, that man is going to pay."

Martha Green made arrangements to have her husband buried on the ranch, at the foot of the big pine tree. This confirmed in her mind that there was no way she would ever leave those acres up along Bullis Creek. In her mind this ranch would remain in the Green name forever.

Dan stood off to one side as two of the town's ministers said words over the casket. Jack and Martha had divided their religious beliefs between two denominations and both had been asked to represent the final rites.

Martha was dressed in a dark blue riding outfit with a black veil down over her face. Next to her, dressed in a black riding outfit with thin white trim, was Lucy Green. She was in her late twenties, slim and of medium height, with hair that was as red as a burning ember. The one time she looked over at Dan, he could see deep green eyes that absorbed everything in a flash. They were eyes that could be soft and beckoning, or as hard as jade stone.

Dan noticed also that Lucy Green wore no veil. Standing close to the coffin, with an arm around her mother, she seemed detached from the whole thing. It was as if she was formulating what was to happen from that day on within her mind. She paid little attention to the words of each minister's sermon and she spent little time with them when the words were finished. She wanted it to be over and to make her moves right away.

Ben Hutton stood next to Lucy. He had recognized Dan immediately. He was wearing a trim-cut beige western suit that seemed to make his light blond features paler than they normally would have been. Even his hat was light colored, making his blue eyes seem pale and ineffective.

Friends and relatives stood around for a short time after the coffin was lowered. Dan approached

Martha and Lucy and offered his sympathies to both of them.

"This is my daughter Lucy," Martha said to Dan. "I've already mentioned her to you before."

"Yes, you have," Dan said. "It's a pleasure." Lucy offered her hand and Dan took it.

"And this is Ben Hutton," Martha added. "You already mentioned that you two were acquainted."

Dan took Ben Hutton's hand and Ben smiled thinly. He was a man who liked to hoard the attention if he could, wherever he might be. But he knew that when Dan Slayter was around, no one noticed very many others.

"Good to see you again, Ben," Dan said. "It's been a number of years since we took those dudes up into the Scapegoat."

Ben tried to smile again. "It's been awhile, hasn't it. But I see you've made yourself the authority. That's good, isn't it?"

"I like it," Dan said. "I like it just fine."

"Are you making any headway in learning what happened to my father?" Lucy asked.

"I don't know if this is the time or place to discuss this with you," Dan said, "but I know you're anxious to learn where things are."

"We are both very anxious to learn what happened," Martha said. "What have you found out?"

"There were a number of other men besides Jack who were on the mountain that night," Dan said. "That means there was likely a fight. There is no evidence to support who else was up there at this time."

"You know who was up there," Lucy said quickly. "It was Big Jed Barlow and his Cross Twelve hands."

"Even if it was Jed Barlow," Dan said, "I have no evidence that can positively link him to your father's death. Do you understand that?"

"I think I understand that Jed Barlow operates outside the law and that he's good at it," Lucy said. "Mother and I have been doing some talking and we've agreed that Jed Barlow will now try as hard as he can to get this ranch. But we aren't going to give this place up for anything, and we'll fight together to keep what is ours. If that means we have to kill Jed Barlow, then we will."

"I can understand your anger," Dan told Lucy. "But like I told your mother the other day, killing Jed Barlow will only bring you more grief than you already have."

"It's important that you understand how serious we are about keeping this ranch," Martha spoke up. "That's all we are saying. Lucy and I will be here when Jed Barlow is gone. And Ben as well, if that's what he and Lucy decide."

"I intend to finish the rodeo circuit this summer and marry Lucy," Ben put in. "Maybe you didn't know, but I'm doing some work as a stock detective as well. I think I can find out what happened up on that mountain."

"Finding out and acting on it are two different things," Dan pointed out. "Whatever Big Jed Barlow did will have to be taken care of by my office."

"Sheriff Slayter, that man killed my father,"

Lucy then said. "He won't get away with it."

"There has to be proof that he killed your father," Dan said again. "You all have to remember that."

"I know from the way mother described what went on that Big Jed Barlow was stealing our cattle and my father caught him in the act," Lucy said. "They had to get rid of him."

Dan looked back and forth from Lucy to Martha. Both women were determined to set things straight. Ben Hutton was standing with them, certain he was going to be there for them and do his part.

"I have a score to settle with Big Jed Barlow myself," Hutton said suddenly. "He swindled me out of a prize horse one time. I haven't forgotten that."

"There are a lot of people who dislike the Barlows and the Cross Twelve Ranch," Dan said. "But there has to be a case against them before they can be tried for anything in a court of law. You all understand that. Getting evidence is what matters here—not just going off after the Barlows."

"Well, you'd better know that I'm going to help Martha and Lucy all I can with this problem," Hutton said. "We all know it's the Barlows who are causing the trouble. And they are responsible for Jack Green's death. I'm going to make sure they pay for it."

"You had better be sure just how far you can go with this little threat," Dan told Hutton. "If you break the law, you'll be behind bars just as fast as

49

the next person."

Hutton stared at Dan a moment without speaking. Finally he said, "It looks to me like you're taking the Cross Twelve's side in this thing."

"Don't try to make little games out of this thing, Hutton," Dan said. "You're not going to convince anybody that I'm taking sides. I have a job to do and that's what I'm here for. If the Cross Twelve is breaking the law, then Big Jed Barlow and all the rest of them will go to jail. And if you break the law, you'll be in there with them."

Hutton walked off by himself and looked out over the bottom toward Canyon Mountain. Dan knew that he was going to have to be careful about this case, as Ben Hutton was good at stirring up emotions. He had always been that way, and usually the emotions were anger and rebellion.

What worried Dan most about Ben Hutton being here was the impression he would make on Martha Green. Dan was certain that Martha Green was going to be under tremendous stress and that Ben Hutton wouldn't help that at all. Hutton already had her thinking he was a hero of some kind, and that he would be good for Lucy. All of that was going to make working with Martha Green that much harder—since Ben Hutton didn't care for him at all.

Dan could see that Lucy was strong and that she would help her mother. But how much she could help her mother depended entirely on how much she cared about Ben Hutton. How far Hutton would go to try and make things work for him was yet to be seen. But Dan knew Hutton would work hard until he got what he wanted — and that was Lucy Green and the ranch.

Chapter Five

Dan watched Ben Hutton as he kicked a boot through the dirt a way off from where he and Lucy and Martha stood. Hutton was still mad about being challenged. Dan knew he wasn't wrong about Ben Hutton and his intentions to have things the way he wanted them. He just wasn't sure how far Lucy would let things go.

"Sheriff Slayter, I don't know you very well," Lucy then said, "but I understand you're a fair and reasonable man, and that you've made this county a safe place to live for most people. But it's not going to be safe on Canyon Mountain until Jed Barlow and his hands realize they have to stay on their side of the fence."

Dan turned his attention back from Hutton. "I intend to talk to Jed Barlow," he said. "I think I can find out a lot about what's going on up here when I meet him face-to-face."

"He won't tell you anything," Martha said. "What makes you think he will?"

"I can learn a lot from a man by just looking at

him," Dan said. "It isn't what he says necessarily that counts; it's how he says it."

Lucy was watching Dan with more and more interest. There was something about Dan that fascinated her—something that reminded her of her father.

Though Lucy had always loved her father, she had never gotten really close to him. He was totally independent and so was she. They never really quarreled all that much, as her father was never one to force what he wanted on anybody. Lucy had thought more than once that had her father been somewhat more forceful, Big Jed Barlow might have had a harder time ruining the Green Ranch.

But somehow Lucy always knew she would be the one making most of the decisions on the ranch. She had left for college when most women her age had been graduated for two or three years. Now she had a degree in rangeland management and was looking forward to operating the ranch in such a way that there would be good grass for the cattle all year around. And in her mind, that was going to be a reality—whatever it took to stop Big Jed Barlow.

She had met and fallen in love with Ben Hutton her second year in college. He had been riding in a rodeo at Three Forks and she had gotten to know him at a party. Lucy was herself fairly well known in the rodeo circuit. She had a big palomino named Lady that she had trained to race around barrels and she had won good money at it. There were those who said this season could be her best ever.

Since meeting in Three Forks, Lucy and Ben Hutton had been going together off and on ever since then. But Lucy had been wondering more and more if making the relationship permanent wasn't a mistake. The more she was around Hutton the more she realized he wasn't all he tried to be. In fact, he wasn't anything near what he tried to be.

That had been on Lucy's mind for some time and she had been going to tell Ben that she was no longer interested in seeing him as much. Then the word of her father's death came and she didn't know how to tell him. He seemed so sincere about wanting to help her get things together on the ranch with her mother. He said he would help in any way he could. The one thing Lucy did know was that she didn't want to see the ranch fail.

And keeping the ranch was now foremost on Lucy Green's mind. It angered her deeply to know that Big Jed Barlow and the Cross 12 Ranch had taken her father's life. Now the Barlows wanted the ranch for their own, and she would never allow it. She wanted Dan to know this.

"There is one thing that you should be aware of, Sheriff Slayter," she told Dan. "Laws or no laws, Mother and I will never allow Big Jed Barlow to ever own this ranch—never!"

"Don't you think I can do my job as sheriff of this county?" Dan asked her.

"Yes, I think you can do your job well," Lucy

answered. "We've heard about you and how you've gone up into the wilderness after people nobody could capture. But Jed Barlow is a different story."

"How is he so different?" Dan asked. "People who want to break the law and are the smart ones usually do it for the money that's in it. Barlow is that kind. He's greedy. Sooner or later he'll get too greedy and forget to use good judgment. Then he'll go to jail."

Lucy thought for a moment. She asked her mother how she was feeling and Martha replied that she was fine. Then Lucy turned back to Dan.

"We just want Big Jed Barlow to pay for what he did to my father," Lucy said.

"Barlow will pay for any crimes he might have committed," Dan promised. "I'll see to that. If Jed Barlow did kill your father and it was no accident, I'll get the evidence I need to bring Barlow in. Give me the time to do it and your troubles will be over."

"You're going to have your hands full getting anything on Barlow," Martha said. "And as for Lucy and I, it seems it will be some time yet before our troubles are over. In fact, I have a feeling they're just starting."

Brice Foster poured alcohol into the bullet hole in his arm and winced. Jack Green had managed to hit him with one of the bullets he had fired in rapid succession from his .30-06. Though Big Jed Barlow had the rifle now, Foster was the one who had sustained the injury, and all the plans he had had for getting the job done for Barlow and heading for Nevada had crashed.

Before the helicopter pilot had managed to drive Jack Green and his horse off the cliff, Green had managed to disrupt their operation to the point that they could get only one of the bulls. There was one bull left, and that would be a hard one to get. And Foster had made a deal with Big Jed Barlow to get paid after the last bull was rustled.

Foster had told Big Jed about the possibility that Jack Green could be trouble. But Barlow thought he could handle everybody, especially Jack Green. Barlow had kept saying that Green was just one man—but just one man can spoil a lot of plans made by a lot of men.

But now there was no more Jack Green, and that brought on additional problems. That meant there would be a sheriff named Dan Slayter looking into everything. That wasn't good, as he was no ordinary sheriff. Everyone knew that. He would stay on a case until he had it solved. He never quit.

And that was what bothered Brice Foster a lot right now. Foster knew he had lost the syringe and vial that he had given the bull the shot with. He couldn't find it in his coat pocket and he knew he had lost it up in the grass when Jack Green was shooting at him. If Dan Slayter found the vial, he would soon know who was doing the rustling for Big Jed Barlow.

Next to Big Jed Barlow was his younger brother,

Chet. Now Chet Barlow stood nearby watching Foster dab the wound with the alcohol. He wondered at Foster's grit; most anyone else would have screamed their head off. Big Jed was watching also. He was not so much concerned with Foster or the wound as he was with the missing vial. Foster had emptied his pockets twice and had not found it. This concerned Big Jed a great deal, as it was tangible evidence against Foster if anyone found the vial. And it wouldn't be just anyone who might find it—the chances were it would be Dan Slayter.

Big Jed Barlow did not know Dan Slayter all that well; he had only spoken to the man once when there had been a brawl outside one of Clark City's bars—one of the few brawls Big Jed had managed to keep himself out of. At the time, Slayter had merely asked him if he knew either of the two men lying unconscious on the sidewalk. Big Jed had said no and walked away.

That one impression was enough to tell Big Jed that Dan Slayter wasn't afraid of anybody. Most people couldn't look Big Jed in the eye, but Big Jed looked straight into Dan Slayter's steady dark eyes that day and Slayter hadn't even considered wincing. What there was about this young sheriff was baffling, but Big Jed knew this man wouldn't back down from something he started out to do.

"There's only one thing to do, Foster," Big Jed finally said. "And that's go back up on Canyon Mountain and find that vial. That's the only way to keep it from being found by Slayter."

"That's crazy," Foster blurted. He was wrapping his arm with a cut of old white cloth. "There's no way I could ever find that little vial up there, not in a week of Sundays. Besides, what if I go back up there and somebody catches me? Then there'll be trouble for sure. I say we just take our chances. The odds are Slayter won't find that vial."

Big Jed was still pacing the floor. "You had better hope to hell he doesn't," Big Jed finally said. "It's got your fingerprints all over it. And if Slayter comes out here looking for you, I'll tell him you don't work here no more. And guess what? That won't be no lie, either."

Foster looked hard at Big Jed and frowned. "You just give me my cut of the money for that bull and I'll be out of here. Give me the money now and I'm gone."

Big Jed put his hands. "Not so fast, Foster. I didn't mean to rile you. I think you're right. I don't see how anyone could find that vial up there in all that grass. Just rest easy."

Foster finished wrapping his arm and taping the cloth in place without another word. When he was done, he clomped out of the ranch house and out to the corrals, where he saddled a horse and rode off.

"Where do you suppose he's headed?" Chet asked Big Jed.

Big Jed shrugged. "Maybe up on top. I don't know. But one thing I do know, you and he had better start getting along."

"Why are you telling me?" Chet said defensively.

"He's the one who's the smart-ass. Ever since he came here and started changing brands on Green Ranch cattle, he's acted like the class dandy. And you encourage him. What the hell are you telling me to straighten up for?"

Big Jed took note of his brother's anger. He realized the friction was getting worse and that Chet had a point: Foster was a bit hard to take. But he was entitled to his attitude; he was, after all, the best at changing brands there ever was.

"I'll talk to him," Big Jed finally said. "But I just wanted you to know that we've got to stick together. If Slayter finds that vial, all hell could break loose."

"Maybe you'd better have Foster hide out for a time," Chet suggested. "Send him up to the Diamond Six on the Flathead for a while. If Slayter can't find him here, maybe he'll give up."

Big Jed thought a moment. "That's a good idea. Maybe I'll ship Foster up there for a while, until this all cools down some. But if Slayter found that vial, we're going to have to figure something out. My guess is he'll come out here and he won't find Foster, but that won't stop him. I doubt if Dan Slayter will give up."

Dan stood in the office with Leon, studying the results of the lab tests on the plastic vial. The blood was human, and the fingerprints belonged to a man named Brice Foster. He had served time in Nevada and Oregon both for armed robbery and stealing horses. He had been a member of a gang of thieves stealing wild horses from the Nevada desert and selling them to the canneries for dog food.

This evidence served to pinpoint one of the hands Big Jed Barlow had hired to help him steal Green Ranch livestock. Big Jed had gotten the best he could find for his dirty dealings against the Greens. But the problem was, it did nothing to help get Barlow behind bars. Since the blood on the vial couldn't have come from the bull, Dan wondered about its true source. The chances were better than ever that the blood belonged to Brice Foster.

"Since it seems so certain that this Brice Foster is working for the Cross Twelve Ranch," Dan said to Leon, "I think it would be a good idea if we took a little spin out there and talked to this Mr. Foster."

"Are we going to take him in?" Leon asked.

"We haven't got enough for that," Dan said. "But I would like to hear what he has to say about his fingerprints on this vial, as well as the blood."

The drive out to the Cross 12 was pleasant, warm enough for Dan to lower the top on his Jeep. The Yellowstone and all the streams running down into it were filled with fly fishermen cashing in on the late salmon fly hatch. There were campers and trailers everywhere up and down the highway, and more coming in off the interstate.

Leon remarked that he wished he owned a sporting goods shop for just a couple of months

60

out of the summer—preferably May and June—so that he could retire. He realized that the overhead and slow business of the first few months of each year sucked all the profits out of the stores. He was interested in just the best months and not the worst.

"That would sure be the best way to do things, wouldn't it?" Dan said with a laugh. "Own a department store during the Christmas rush, and then let somebody else have it during the summer while everybody was out fishing. During the warm season, you could own the fishing and tackle shacks. Not a bad way to go."

Leon nodded. "The way we have it now is no matter what the season, it's always rush-rush and we don't get paid for it."

"Yes, but you love your work," Dan said.

"Yes, I wake up at night in a cold sweat just thinking about it," Leon said. "I just can't wait to get my ass shot off."

"It's not getting your ass shot off that's so bad," Dan pointed out. "It's when they put it back together that really hurts."

They turned off the highway and took the gravel road up the north side of Wineglass Mountain to the end. The ranch was large and the buildings were many and spread out. But the paint was fading and there was a lot of junk just sitting around, as if it had just been dropped and left.

Pinning Big Jed Barlow down for the death of Jack Green was not going to be an easy task. Even if they succeeded in finding Brice Foster and learning that he worked for the Cross 12, that still would make any of the Barlows worry. They could just say Foster was acting on his own.

Anything the Barlows wanted to do right next to Canyon Mountain would not incriminate them. Canyon Mountain was just adjacent to Wineglass Mountain and since the Cross 12 owned all of Wineglass Mountain and everything on all sides of it, any tracks in that area—even if they were coming from Canyon Mountain—could have been made legitimately by Cross 12 hands out checking cattle.

Dan knew he would have to catch the Barlows in the act of rustling to really have anything on them. But it didn't hurt to see what they were up to and see how many lies Big Jed could tell. Nobody ever got much more than a lie out of Big Jed Barlow. And in a situation like this, he would be in top form.

Dan realized Foster was likely gone from the ranch by now—sent somewhere to hide out. It was certain that Foster would be hard to locate. Still, just being out at the Cross 12 would make Big Jed and his brother, Chet, worry about their efforts to take over the Green Ranch. And it would let them know that the law was breathing down their necks.

Chapter Six

Dan and Leon found themselves in the Cross 12 Ranch yard, with two pit bull terrier dogs barking and growling at them. Dan could see Big Jed and Chet both standing on the porch. There some other hands standing nearby as well. They were all watching the pit bull terriers get ready to go at Dan's Jeep. Neither Big Jed nor Chet made any moves to call the dogs off, but seemed amused.

One of the pit bulls rushed the Jeep and tried to jump up to get in the window at Dan. It jumped and snapped and growled, showing long white teeth. Dan pulled his pistol and cocked it.

"Thrasher! Come back here!"

It was Big Jed's voice and he came down off the porch in a hurry, before Dan had a chance to shoot. He sent both dogs inside and turned back to Dan and Leon, with his face in a snarl.

"You would've shot my dog, wouldn't you?" he said.

"Blame yourself for that, Barlow," Dan said, getting out of the Jeep. "If you haven't got enough sense to keep those dogs under control, you don't deserve to have them."

Leon got out of the other side, aware of the eyes that watched him closely. He could see some of the hands whispering to one another.

Then Chet walked down off the porch. "I don't think the dogs much care for your deputy," he said. "I think that's what the problem is."

Leon was used to that kind of remark and it didn't bother him in the least. Instead he chuckled.

"I don't think they worry about me that much," Leon said to Chet. "But I notice when they're around you, they keep their tails tucked tight down over their assholes."

Chet straightened and took a step forward. Leon kept grinning. Chet stopped at the edge of the porch and the sun shone on the hard lines in his face.

"What did you just say?" he asked.

"I said your dogs had better sleep a long way from you," Leon answered.

Chet turned to Big Jed. "They can't come out here and insult us like that."

Big Jed put a hand up to calm his brother. Then he turned to Dan.

"We really don't like having you out here," he said. "What do you want?"

"We don't like being out here any more than you like having us out," Dan told Big Jed. "So let's get to the point. Jack Green went off a cliff and it happened while he was up on Canyon Mountain chasing someone who was rustling his cattle. Know anything about that?"

64

"We ain't done nothing wrong," Big Jed said suddenly.

"Did I say that?" Dan asked. "I just asked you if you knew anything about it."

"No, we don't know anything about it. So why don't you just get the hell out of here."

Dan pulled Brice Foster's photo from the file and showed it to both Barlows. Though they tried to hide their expressions, Dan could tell they knew Foster well.

"Who is that and what does he have to do with us?" Big Jed asked.

"Don't play games with me," Dan said flatly. "This man works for you changing brands on other people's cattle. He left his fingerprints on a little plastic vial up on Canyon Mountain. There was some blood on that vial, too, though I don't know if it was his or someone else's. Which brings me back to the subject of Jack Green."

"That was too bad," Big Jed said with no expression. "But I already said we didn't have anything to do with him."

"That's not what Martha Green says." Dan was watching Big Jed's expression closely now. "She says you've been cutting fences and stealing cattle from the Green Ranch. I don't know why she would lie."

Big Jed started to show his anger. His face pinched up and became red. He wanted to shout at Dan like he did his brother and his hired hands. But he knew better.

"You got no right coming up here and treating

me this way," Big Jed finally said. "I told you, we don't know nothing about Jack Green or any of that."

"But Brice Foster does," Dan said. "And I know he works for you. Where is he? We want to talk to him."

"Foster quit two days ago," Big Jed lied. "He didn't say why. He just said he was moving on."

"So you're telling me that Brice Foster isn't here?" Dan asked.

Big Jed nodded. "That's what I'm telling you."

"Did he steal any cattle while he was here?"

"None that I know of. I don't know where he is now. You'll have to find him and ask him what you want to know."

Dan nodded. He turned to Leon and they both got back into the Jeep. The dogs were again barking at the screen door as Dan and Leon drove out of the yard without looking back at the Barlows. He headed the Jeep toward town, the expression on his face set firmly.

"What are you going to do about them?" Leon asked, "They were lying through their teeth."

"I know they were," Dan said. "And I intend to prove it. I'm convinced that Big Jed Barlow will do anything he can to get the Green Ranch. I just hope we can stop him before it's too late."

Brice Foster walked the grounds of the Diamond 6 Ranch. The Flathead Valley was a pretty place from all aspects, but under the circumstances he couldn't enjoy the scenery.

His gunshot wound troubled him, even though he was taking more than the prescribed amount of pain killers. A doctor had been brought to the ranch and the man hadn't said one word to him during the entire process of dressing the wound. Foster was sure the man was paid generously to care for any number of injuries at this ranch in this manner and that he was just another number on the doctor's list of secret patients.

Foster wasn't sure how long he was going to have to be here. He hadn't planned on such an extensive stay in Montana. He had been told by Big Jed Barlow that the rustling job on the Green Ranch would be simple and easy. But Foster realized he should never consider anything in his business simple and easy.

All during the last week since his arrival, Foster had been anxious to leave. He knew his wound would take at least another two to three weeks to heal properly. But Foster was anxious to get the rustling job over with and get back down to Nevada. Sore arm or not, he could get the work done.

But Big Jed Barlow had other ideas. He was a clever man and overly cautious at times, to Foster's way of thinking. Barlow called nearly every day and not long ago he had told Foster that the sheriff, Dan Slayter, had come out to the Cross 12 Ranch with a black deputy, and they had been snooping around. Foster had learned from Barlow that Slayter and the deputy had found the vial and were looking for the man who had dropped it.

"You just stay put right where you are," Barlow had told Foster in finishing the conversation. "If you want to find yourself in jail, just come back here. Slayter is hot on your trail."

Foster kept thinking of himself as some kind of fool now. He was hiding out, some kind of wanted criminal, while it was Big Jed Barlow who stood to gain from the whole operation: he could have an entire ranch when the last of those expensive bulls was hauled away. That would amount to a great deal of money, as he would certainly be able to take over the ranch after the bank foreclosed at a low price per acre.

The more Foster thought about it, the more angered he became. It didn't matter to him that this ranch setup was tied in with the Cross 12, and that he would have everything he wanted whenever he wanted it—including women. What Foster wanted was the ability to come and go as he pleased. He had never had to stay in one place so long in his life. He didn't know if he could get used to it.

He had already gotten resentful of Big Jed Barlow's calls. He knew Barlow could care less about how his arm felt, but was concerned whether or not he was staying at the ranch. Foster could have told him he had no reason to worry—that it wouldn't be smart to just take off, not and leave behind a large sum of money that he was owed for doing the work on the other Charolais bulls. But Barlow wanted to keep calling.

Foster rarely said much to Barlow at all during the conversations; he just wanted them over. But the day Barlow called about adding to his work load, Foster grew angry and all his resentment overflowed.

"I think you could stay in practice working on brands if you wanted to do a little work for the Diamond Six," Barlow began. "They've got some stock coming in day after tomorrow."

Foster grunted over the phone. "How much extra am I getting for it?" he asked.

There was a silence at the other end of the phone. Finally, Foster heard Big Jed Barlow say something.

"We can work that out later."

"No," Foster said, "we can work that out now."

"Why are you so edgy?"

"Why do you think? You've got me cooped up here like some school kid and now you want me to stick my neck out up here and change some brands—and you say we'll work the money out later. What the hell kind of fool do you play me for?"

"Didn't mean to rile you," Barlow said. "I just thought you'd like to do some work—keep your fingers from getting so itchy."

"My fingers get itchy when I hear the sound of money," Foster said.

"Then let's talk money," Barlow said. "Better yet, I'll have them pay you the same as what you're getting per head here."

"Regular cattle or expensive bulls?" Foster asked.

"No expensive bulls," Barlow said. "Some registered cattle, worth good money, but no bulls. Talk to a hand named Rusty up there. Tell him to call me to make arrangements."

"But I'm not that interested in working up here," Foster said. "I want to finish that job for you and get out of state."

"You're already up there," Barlow said. "Why not make good use of your time?"

"Let me get this figured out," Foster said. "If I'm healed up enough to work on brands up here, I'm well enough to go back down and get that last bull taken care of, don't you think?"

"The time's not right," Barlow said. "Slayter is still nosing around and he's got deputies checking out the country all around here. If you were to come back right away, you'd be in jail. You don't want that."

"And you don't either," Foster pointed out. "You might as well level with me, Barlow. You're in this as deep as I am. You just don't want to admit it."

"I just want that last Green Ranch bull off Canyon Mountain and you back down in Nevada," Barlow said. "But that can't happen just yet. When are you going to get that through your skull?"

"I'm taking chances up here," Foster argued. "Why not just go down there and take the chances?"

"Nobody up there has a vial with your finger-prints on it," Barlow answered. "If you don't want to believe me when I tell you they want you in jail down here, then I'll send you a paper. Your picture is on the front page."

"My picture?" Foster was shocked. "My picture is on the front page of the paper?"

Barlow cleared his throat. "I wouldn't be too proud. The photo looks like a mug shot to me."

"I just want out of here," Foster finally said. "I just want to finish the work for you and get out of here."

"That will make us both plenty happy," Barlow said. "In the meantime, you're going to have to take my word for how bad things are down here. Just because Jack Green went over that cliff doesn't mean Dan Slayter thinks it was an accident. He wants to throw somebody in jail."

Foster took a deep breath. "How long do you think it will be until I can get back down there?"

"At least another three to four weeks," Barlow answered. "It's going to take that long to let the air clear around here. Slayter won't give up easy."

"I still think I can hide out up in the Beartooth for a while," Foster said. "That way I would be closer and we could get that last bull shipped out sooner."

"I've told you, Foster, I don't want to take any chances." Barlow was getting a strong tone to his voice now. "You can't take Dan Slayter lightly. He knows all the tricks and he'll be watching."

Foster was silent for a time. He knew Barlow

was right; if he went back to Clark City or anywhere close, Slayter would likely find him given enough time. It was smarter to hide out somewhere distant from River County and wait for the investigation of Jack Green's death to blow over.

Finally, Foster agreed to remain at the Diamond 6 until he got the word from Barlow that he could come back to River County and get the last rustling job done. Foster realized he hadn't any choice if he wanted his money for the work he had already done for Barlow. He was stuck where he was for the time being.

Foster hung up the phone and paced around outside of the ranch house for a while. It made him nervous to think he was wanted that badly by Dan Slayter. The more he thought about it, the more it bothered him. Barlow was right — he should sit tight for a time.

Finally, Foster decided he would change some brands for the Diamond 6 to keep in practice. He would find the ranch hand they called Rusty and tell him to call Barlow. He could use some extra money, if the Diamond 6 was willing to pay it, and he wanted to be ready to change the brand on that Green Ranch bull as fast as he could. If he was going to be up here for another month, he at least wanted to be ready to work fast when he got back to River County.

Chapter Seven

Big Jed Barlow hung up the phone after talking with Brice Foster and cursed. It was always frustrating to talk to Foster and since he had to check up on things at the Diamond 6 on a daily basis, it was driving him crazy.

"I just don't know how much longer I can stand this," Big Jed said. He paced the floor of the living room in the ranch house and had his servant fix him a large whiskey.

"I don't know what to think of Foster now," Big Jed said to Chet. He took the drink from the servant. "We can't depend on him. But he's the best. He can change brands like nobody else."

Chet was watching his older brother fret over Foster. It was true that Foster was one-of-a-kind when it came to changing brands, but the man was also a fool—and crazy as well. There was no telling what he would do now that he had to wait for a time to let his wound heal.

What had started out as simple had suddenly become very complicated. The effort to get the Green Ranch had gone well for a long time; but now the last steps were going to be the hardest.

Chet knew how badly Big Jed wanted this over with. And he knew how important it was to Big Jed to have Foster involved. But Chet didn't think they needed Foster to rustle the last bull off the Green Ranch property. Chet's view was to just forget about Foster.

"Think about it," Chet said. "He may be the best, but he can cause us more trouble than he's worth. You knew before you hired him that he's unstable. I warned you."

"Oh, I don't want to hear that anymore!" Barlow yelled. He spilled half the drink on the carpet and yelled for the servant to clean it up. "All I ever hear from you is 'I told you so . . . I told you so.' Enough of that. I'm sick of it."

"Maybe you ought to listen to me more often," Chet said. "At least we wouldn't be in all these predicaments."

"How the hell do you know that?" Barlow asked Chet. He pushed the servant away from the mess on the carpet and told him to fix him another drink.

"If we keep these jobs just inside the family, we're a lot better off," Chet said. "Every time we bring in somebody from the outside, something like this happens."

"Who was to know Jack Green would come riding up there the other night?" Barlow asked. "I call it bad luck, nothing more."

"And I'm saying you're going to have more bad luck if you don't get rid of Foster," Chet argued.

"He might be the best at changing brands, but he's also the worst at using his head."

"He's just a little crazy, that's all," Big Jed said in Foster's defense. "He can work on that. He can do us a lot of good."

"You keep letting the good overshadow the bad," Chet pointed out. "If you were looking at things clearly, you would see that Foster has caused a whole lot more trouble than he's worth."

Big Jed turned quickly. "You're just saying that because you're jealous of him."

"I have a right to be," Chet said quickly. "When he's around, you favor him over me. I don't like that."

"He just wants to be considered special," Big Jed said. "He's worth it."

"How much am I worth?" Chet asked. "I'm your brother, for Christ's sake."

Big Jed slurped on his drink. He avoided looking at Chet while he talked.

"I know that. I just want this thing to come off right. I want the Green Ranch, and that means making Brice Foster happy until we get that last bull. Don't take it personal."

"Well, I *am* taking it personal," Chet said. "Foster is causing a lot of trouble between us, and a lot of trouble in general."

"It will be over soon," Big Jed promised. "When Foster gets back, we'll finish up on Canyon Mountain and he'll go back to Nevada."

"Are you sure he's not going to cause us more trouble?" Chet wondered. "What if he gets back here and all hell breaks loose?"

Big Jed paced the floor for a while longer, thinking about what Chet was asking. Chet thought Foster could make things worse for them than they already were. Big Jed had to admit that his brother had a good point. But the Green Ranch was just too tempting to pass up—and Foster was the key to success.

Big Jed downed another drink and went to one of the windows to look out over Canyon Mountain.

"I want that pasture up there," he said, slurring his words. "I want the Green Ranch to be part of the Cross Twelve, and I'm going to see that it is."

"Then think about doing it smart," Chet said. "Think about working it around Foster and not necessarily with him."

Big Jed turned from the window. "What do you mean?"

"I mean we can use Foster. But we have to do it someplace but up on Canyon Mountain—someplace but here in this county. We'll be taking a big chance if we bring him back here. I'm telling you, Jed, we'll be sorry if he shows up here again."

Big Jed was still watching Chet intently. "What you got in mind?"

Chet started out slowly, as he always did when he wanted to convince his older brother of something. "I think if we can get that last Charolais bull down off Canyon Mountain, we'll have things our way. We can haul that bull up into the Flathead and let Foster work on the brand at the Diamond

Six. That way we don't have to take any chances having Foster back down here again."

"I don't know," Big Jed argued. "We're taking a hell of a chance moving a bull worth that much money around without first changing the brand. If we got caught, we'd have no way of saying the bull was ours. At least if Foster was here to change the brand right away, nobody could say it was a Green Ranch bull."

"If we set it up right, we can make it work," Chet said. "It would take only one night, then it would be all over. And it would be all over for the Green Ranch, too." He laughed.

Big Jed worked on another drink. He paced back and forth for a time and finally asked Chet how to make it work.

"We don't have to be in a real big rush," Chet said. "We can pick the right night, call in the helicopter, then truck the bull up to the Flathead and have Foster change the brand. We don't have to tell Foster the bull is coming. Just show up. That way Foster won't be going crazy."

Big Jed nodded. "That sounds good. As it is, Foster thinks he is going to be working on cattle for the Diamond Six until I tell him different. He won't have any idea we're going up on the mountain to get that bull. That should work. But I'm still worried about Dan Slayter."

"Forget about Slayter," Chet said. "He's got nothing on anybody but Foster. With Foster out of here, we don't have to worry. Besides, when the bull is gone it will be all over. The bank will have to foreclose on the Green Ranch and we end up with the property."

Big Jed was smiling. It all sounded so good — and so simple. All they had to do was pick the right night to go up on Canyon Mountain. Then the Green Ranch would belong to them.

Lucy was setting barrels up inside the largest of the corrals. She had been working with Lady for nearly a week, limbering up the horse's muscles and getting the palomino in shape for the grueling work of racing.

During this time, she was finding herself having a great deal of fun. Despite the fact that the Barlows and the Cross 12 Ranch were just waiting for the chance to take over, Lucy was seeing that she could help keep the ranch by making money with her horse.

Ben Hutton had been watching all this as well. Lucy had not slept with him since their arrival at the ranch and this bothered him. She had told him they would stay in separate bedrooms out of respect for her mother. This was all right, but he thought they should be able to take advantage of the time when Martha Green went shopping in town.

But Lucy was changing and Hutton could see it clearly. She no longer listened to his stories of rodeo rides and big purses he had won in big cities. Before he got started on the stories, she would ask him to name the rodeo he had participated in and the city it had been held in. She had come to realize he hadn't won any big purses anywhere.

Hutton didn't care anymore if Lucy believed him or not; he had her mother in the palm of his hand. She still believed his stories and encouraged him not to lose faith in Lucy. She would tell him often that Lucy was just going through a stage and that she would soon understand she should settle down and get married.

Hutton decided to try and get back on Lucy's good side by taking a ride up on Canyon Mountain to see if he couldn't make it look like he had found something that would help them against the Barlows. Partway up the mountain he turned back to the ranch. He had gone far enough to make it look good.

He returned well after nightfall. Lucy was at the kitchen table with Martha, but paid him little attention when he came in and slammed the door behind him.

"I know more about what happened up there now than Slayter does," Hutton said. "He can't help you with this thing as much as I can. Where's supper?"

"You weren't here for it," Lucy said. "Everything's put away."

"Oh, now Lucy, don't be so harsh," Martha spoke up. She got up from the table and went to the refrigerator. "There's some roast beef left." She looked to Hutton and smiled. "Let me warm it up for you."

Hutton grinned and took a place at the table.

"Let him warm it up, Mother," Lucy said. "There's nothing wrong with his hands. And he knows how to operate the stove."

"Lucy, now I want to do this for him," Martha insisted. She took a cup from the cupboard and poured Hutton some coffee. "Ben, you just visit with Lucy and the meat will be ready in just a few minutes."

"Any potatoes left over?" Hutton asked.

"Yes, I'll warm them up also," Martha said.

Lucy shook her head. Hutton was still smiling. He sipped on his coffee and worked on Lucy.

"I just told you I could solve your problem with Big Jed Barlow," he said. "Did you hear me?"

"I heard you," Lucy said. "But that doesn't mean I believe you. In fact, I think you're full of shit."

Hutton's eyes widened. "Why did you say that?"

"You can't even get your own meal when you're late for supper," Lucy said. "You have to be waited on. How can I expect you to know what to do in a case as important as Big Jed Barlow?"

"Lucy, your mother *wants* to fix the meal," Hutton said.

"He's right," Martha spoke up. "Why are you being so hard on him?"

Lucy got up from the table and walked outside. The night air from the mountain had cooled the yard down and there was a loud croaking of frogs and chirping of crickets from the darkness beyond. Lucy found it refreshing after the atmosphere inside the house. But her sensations were short-lived, as she heard the door to the house open and Ben Hutton's boots clomping across the yard behind her.

"What the hell's the matter with you, Lucy?" he asked. "You don't even give me the time of day anymore. I want to know what's wrong."

She turned to him, her arms crossed. "Ben, we're not meant for each other. It's time you understand that, since you can't take a hint."

Hutton took a moment to recover. "Why do you think that?" he finally asked.

"I've never taken the time to really get to know you," she said. "Or maybe I only thought I knew you. Now I find that you are somebody who just wants to be a hero to everybody. You really don't care for me. So why pretend?"

Hutton realized Lucy had come to know all about him. It made him nervous, but he realized he still had her mother on his side. He wanted Lucy Green and the Green Ranch. He wasn't going to give up so easily.

"I don't think it's fair to say I don't care about you." Hutton finally told Lucy.

"No you don't," Lucy said. "Otherwise you wouldn't want to make a fool of me in front of my mother."

"Lucy, she *wanted* to cook for me."

"That's not the point. I won't ever give you all the attention you think you need. You think everyone should cater to you all the time. That's not the way it is with me, and you could never get used to that."

81

Hutton looked at her for a moment and finally said, "Ever since you met Slayter, you've been different."

"Don't blame this on Dan Slayter," Lucy said. "You think you need to have everybody around you worship you. I'm sorry to say that I did just that for a long time. But that's over. You've got to take me on equal terms now. Do you think you could ever do that?"

Again Hutton evaded the main issue. He began to talk about all the plans they had made regarding the ranch and how they were going to build it up again together. He fumed about how he had given of his time and now it looked as if that time was going to be wasted.

"I think I'd be better off getting back on the rodeo circuit again," he finally said.

"I think you would, too," Lucy said. "I think you should take your falls in somebody else's arena from now on."

"You're going to be sorry that you treated me like this," Hutton warned.

"I doubt it," Lucy said.

Hutton turned from her and churned his boots through the gravel of the driveway toward his pickup. He got in and slammed the door and sped out.

For a few moments all there was to the night was the loud roar of Ben Hutton's pickup as he lurched his way through the gears toward the main road. He was going as fast as he could on the gravel road without losing full control of the pickup. Lucy was certain he would look for a suitable bar to sulk in.

And she knew that her mother would likely be angry with her for arguing with him. He certainly had her believing he was a top-rate hand. And Lucy didn't know how she was ever going to convince her mother otherwise.

There was the sound of the door to the house opening and Lucy watched her mother come out into the yard.

"Oh, dear," she said. "You've had another argument."

"I'm afraid so," Lucy said. "I hope it's the last one we have—the last time I have to worry about it."

"Where did Ben go?" she asked.

Lucy watched the tail lights of Hutton's pickup finally disappear totally into the darkness. "I guess he didn't feel like having roast beef and mashed potatoes."

Martha shrugged and turned back toward the house. "I'll leave them on the stove," she said. "He might be hungry when he gets back."

Chapter Eight

Lucy had trouble sleeping. During the night, she tossed and turned in her bed and worried that Ben Hutton was going to cause her mother's heart to act up. Her mother was worried about where Hutton had gone and if he was all right.

After thinking about it for some time, Lucy decided she would put up with Hutton until the situation with the Cross 12 Ranch was settled. That meant allowing Ben Hutton to stay and help and think he was going to have her for his own. But she wasn't going to let him sleep with her — not ever again.

Hutton could be around and play hero to her mother if he wanted. He might even help them keep the Barlows from rustling more cattle. After it was all over, she could tell Hutton he wasn't what she wanted in a man — she could tell him that again and make him understand. She hated to play it that way, but she was worried that her mother wouldn't be able to stand the strain.

It seemed certain to Lucy that Ben Hutton would likely return to the ranch and act as if nothing had happened. If she tried to drive him off, he might stay distant for a while or he might play up to her mother. That was his ace in the hole. Lucy realized he was as determined to have her and the ranch as she was determined to send him out of her life.

But that could wait until the Green Ranch was secure from the Barlows. Hutton would likely return, but he might leave if the pressure from the Cross 12 got to be too much. Lucy knew him well enough to realize he wouldn't want to put his life in danger for the ranch—not if the Cross 12 was going to get it anyway.

Whether Hutton was around or not, Lucy was determined to save the Green Ranch. She went to sleep that night confident that when Ben Hutton showed up again—which he certainly would—she could make him understand he could stay on under limited conditions. He would gladly accept that, since he was sure he could get her mother to intercede in his behalf.

Lucy wasn't wrong in thinking he would be back. His pickup showed up around midmorning. Lucy was in the corral with Lady, running the palomino around the barrels. She didn't even bother to stop.

Hutton went into the house and had Martha fix him something to eat before he went out to the corrals. When he came out, Lucy was letting Lady rest for a while. She sat on the horse and watched Hutton climb up onto the poles and take a seat.

"Are you going to the Three Forks rodeo next weekend?" he asked.

"Yes," Lucy answered. "Why do you ask?"

"Because I want to make you a bet," he said. "I'll bet I make more money than you do at that rodeo. You put up a share of this ranch. How's that?"

"And what are you going to put up?" Lucy asked. "What have you got that can equal even a very small share of this ranch?"

"I'll start with my pickup," Hutton said.

"It's not paid off."

Hutton shrugged. "How about if you put up what you own of this ranch and I have to win more money at Three Forks than you, plus I have to get rid of Big Jed Barlow. If Barlow's not around, you won't have any more trouble. Does that sound fair?"

Lucy studied Hutton a moment. "What do you mean 'get rid' of Big Jed Barlow?" she asked.

"Just get him off your back. It doesn't matter how I do it, just so I can prove he won't be bothering you or your mother any longer. What do you say?"

"I'm not sure I like what you're proposing," Lucy said. "I don't want to be any part of a wager where you have to somehow 'get rid' of Big Jed Barlow."

"I thought you were mad at him for your father's death," Hutton said. "You know Barlow was responsible."

"Even so, I don't want to be a part of anything you have planned," she said. "I don't mind if you want to stay around here as a hired hand and work, but I don't want you thinking you have to do something drastic in order to win me over. That is never going to happen."

Hutton took a deep breath. "Then you won't bet me?"

"No," Lucy said. She noticed her mother was coming out of the house toward the corrals. The last thing Lucy wanted to do was have her mother in on a conversation like this. "I've got to work with Lady some more now," she told Hutton. "So, if you will excuse me."

Lucy began putting the horse through the paces once more. But now she was bothered about Ben Hutton and what he was planning to do. It was hard to know just what he had in mind, but she knew very well it wasn't good.

Dan had been working with Leon and his other deputies to try and find the whereabouts of Brice Foster. There was no question that Big Jed Barlow had sent him out of the county and that Foster was hiding out in some remote area. Dan just wanted to know if it was anywhere close.

After an entire week of checking all the locations within the county, Dan finally decided that Foster was well out of the county—for the time being. He knew Barlow would bring Foster back when the time was right. But for now there was no way to work on the case any longer.

Dan realized he would have to tell Lucy and Martha Green that he had reached a dead end for the time being. It wasn't going to be a happy thing to tell them, as they were already certain that Barlow was going to get away with the murder of Jack Green. Having to call a halt to the investigation for the time being would only serve to fortify their belief.

Shutting the investigation down brought up another concern: Ben Hutton might decide to take it upon himself to go after Big Jed Barlow. Although Dan had talked to him before about taking the law into his own hands, Hutton was stubborn. And if he wanted Lucy Green badly enough, he would try and prove himself a hero.

Dan decided he would have Leon look into a rumor that Ben Hutton had been in town the night before and had been shooting off his mouth around the local bars. The word was, he was telling everybody how he was going to get rid of Big Jed Barlow and make things safe for Lucy Green — being she was soon going to marry him.

With all this in mind, Dan made a trip out to the Green Ranch to break the news about stopping the investigation and find out what he could about Lucy and Ben Hutton. He pulled into the yard and parked his Jeep near the corrals.

He noticed Ben Hutton sitting on the corrals watching Lucy work with her horse. Martha had been out watching as well it appeared and now she was just on her way back to the house.

She stopped and Dan talked with her a few moments.

"Are you making any headway with the case

against Big Jed Barlow?" she asked.

"I'm afraid we're at a dead end for now," Dan answered truthfully. "There's no new evidence and Brice Foster is no longer in the county."

Martha breathed a deep sigh. "I just can't understand how a man like Big Jed Barlow can get away with so much for so long. Everyone knows he's crooked and that he's after our ranch, but he always manages to get away with everything."

"I have a theory," Dan said. "It seems to me that Brice Foster is gone until his bullet wound heals up. I've heard enough talk to know that he wasn't killed, but just wounded. If he ever comes back into the county, we'll get him. He's Barlow's right-hand man. Barlow won't move any more until Foster gets back."

"I hope you're right," Martha said. She was looking into the corrals now, watching Lucy run her palomino around the barrels. "I just want everyone to be happy around here, that's all."

Dan noticed Martha's eyes going from Lucy on her horse up to Ben Hutton, who was perched on the corral watching the action—purposely ignoring Dan. It seemed obvious that Martha was worried about Lucy and Hutton's relationship. What Dan couldn't understand yet was if she was worried that it was going to end, or that it was going to continue.

"Let me know, please, if you get any more information about Barlow or Brice Foster," Martha said. "Somebody has to pay for killing my husband."

89

Dan watched her go from the corrals into the house. He wished there was more he could do on the case, but with Foster gone and Big Jed Barlow and all his hands with tight alibis for the night of Jack Green's death, there was nothing he could do.

He turned back to catch Hutton staring at him. Hutton then turned his attention back to Lucy and her palomino. Dan decided to see what he could find out from Hutton and made his way over to the fence. He pulled himself up and swung his legs over to seat himself next to Hutton.

"She does pretty well on that horse, doesn't she?" Dan said.

Hutton grunted. "Is that why you came out here? Did you want to watch her on the horse, or when she gets off it?"

Dan watched Lucy ride and smiled faintly. "You sound to me like a worried man."

Hutton bristled. "Worried about what?"

"You tell me."

"You're the one who brought it up," Hutton said defensively. "What did you mean by that remark?"

"I was talking about Lucy's riding," Dan pointed out. "You made it sound like something else. You tell me why you think I'm a threat to your relationship with Lucy."

"I don't," Hutton lied. "She's been going with me for over a year now. We'll be married before long. Pretty soon you'll be standing on *my* ranch and I'll tell you to get the hell off, you can bet on that."

"As long as you're in a betting mood," Dan said, "what do you want to wager that before it's all over, Lucy tells you to take a hike?"

Hutton glared. He wouldn't meet Dan's stare, but instead leaned away and got ready to get down. But Lucy was riding over and he stayed where he was. She noticed his red face and looked to Dan, then back to Hutton.

"Are you two talking over old times?" she asked Hutton.

"I don't have any 'old times' to talk over with him," Hutton said. "He's just out here passing the time of day."

Dan ignored the remark. "I just wanted to get some more information for the investigation into your father's death," Dan said. "I was just admiring your riding style. You should win some good money this year."

Lucy smiled. "Thank you. I hope so. What is it you would like to know about my father?" She got down from her horse and walked through the gate.

Dan stepped down from the fence and Hutton jumped off and stormed away toward the far corral. He didn't look back.

"He seems real touchy to me," Dan said. "But I guess he and I never did get along too well."

Lucy smiled. Dan could see from the way she was looking at him that she was keeping an open mind. Ben Hutton had no doubt told her a lot of things about their association with the guest ranch at the edge of the Bob Marshall Wilderness Area. Dan realized there was no doubt it was all negative

91

toward him. But he had nothing to hide and he knew Lucy could see that.

"Ben and I just don't have the same philosophy about things," Dan went on. "He's entitled to his own opinions, just like everyone else."

Dan and Lucy watched Hutton open a gate on the far side of the corral. He was obviously going to ride up on Canyon Mountain. He jumped on the horse and took off at a lope toward the trail that led up on top.

"Ben thinks he has something to prove to me," Lucy said. "I don't know why."

"I think he's already proved something to you," Dan said. "Now he just wants to undo it and make things better for himself."

"You are blessed with insight," Lucy told Dan. "How could you tell Ben and I were having problems?"

"You've got to remember," Dan said, "I know Ben Hutton. I am getting to know you and your mother pretty well, and it just seems to me that Ben and you are an unlikely couple. But that's not for me to decide."

"You wouldn't want to see me marry him, would you?" Lucy said. "Why?"

"I'm not going to tell you not to marry Ben Hutton," Dan said immediately. "That's none of my business. All I'm doing is investigating the death of your father. Ben Hutton wants to be a part of your life and this ranch, so that means he's a part of my investigation."

"Why is he so worried about your investigation?" Lucy asked. "Does he have something to hide?"

"He doesn't have a criminal record, if that's what you mean," Dan said. "But he could still have criminal tendencies. What do you think?"

Lucy didn't know whether to tell Dan about the discussion she had just had with Hutton or not. From what Hutton had been saying about 'getting rid' of Big Jed Barlow, she was sure that Hutton could kill someone and not be sorry for it. But she didn't want to get Hutton in trouble, not with her mother so unstable.

"I don't think Ben is all there at times," Lucy finally said. "But I've never seen him violent."

Dan nodded. "Hasn't he ever gotten into any fights? Bronc riders tend to get physical at times."

"There are times when he would like to have fought," Lucy said. "But he would have gotten his lights punched out, so he backed off."

Dan nodded again. It seemed to fit: Hutton was likely a very frustrated man, since he couldn't have the glory he wanted and now it looked like he wasn't going to get the woman he wanted. Hutton was the type who might just go crazy at any given moment.

"You and Ben must have had some altercations when you worked together," Lucy said.

"We did," Dan said. "I don't know him that well but I'm sure that he's uncomfortable with how you feel about him right now so he's using me as an excuse for what's happening. There's nothing I can do about that."

"Do you think Ben is who he says he is?" Lucy asked.

"I know who he is," Dan said. "But somebody else might see him differently. I can't interfere with that. Do you understand?"

"You really don't judge people, do you?" Lucy said.

"I can't afford to," Dan told her. "I have to listen to both sides of every story to do my job right. Nothing ever evens out until you weigh both sides."

Lucy nodded. "That's a good attitude to have. So how do you weigh my father's death?"

"I think he went up on the mountain looking to stop what was going on up there and found himself overwhelmed," Dan said. "I think he was angry and didn't use good judgment in trying to take on Big Jed Barlow and his hands all by himself. Somehow he got run over that cliff up there, likely by the helicopter. But there's no way I can prove that at this time in a court of law. And I can't bring anybody in without evidence."

Lucy was toying with the reins, twirling them in a circle while she thought. Hutton was now just a black speck in the distance along the trail up Canyon Mountain. Finally Lucy took a deep breath and just looked at Dan.

Dan was silent for a moment. It appeared to him as if Lucy had made up her mind about something, and he couldn't tell if it pertained to Ben Hutton or the situation with the death of her father.

"I don't know how to help you right now," Dan finally said. "I'm sorry I can't pursue Big Jed Barlow, but I have no evidence against him. He's smart. But he'll make a mistake."

Lucy continued to toy with the reins. "And I suppose you want me to relax — to just sit back and let things take their natural course."

"I don't see any other way," Dan said.

"It's really amazing," Lucy then said. "Big Jed Barlow is trying to gulp up our ranch and there's nobody willing to stop him from doing it. My mother wants me to marry a man who's more insecure than she is, and now you're wondering if I think things are going to be fine."

"Things will be fine," Dan promised. "But you're going to have to work with me, not against me."

"I'm going to work for myself," Lucy said. "I'm going to work for myself and my mother — because I want this ranch to remain in our name. Whatever you do for us, we will appreciate. But we're going to keep the ranch, thank you. And maybe Ben Hutton will have to help us."

Lucy got back on her palomino and rode back into the corral. She let the horse run around the barrels and Dan moved back to his Jeep. He left knowing full well that Ben Hutton was going to do what he could to prove himself, and that now was his big moment.

Chapter Nine

Ben Hutton had been gone for three days before he finally called Lucy. He said he was on the rodeo circuit once again, and he promised Lucy he would win some big purses at some major rodeos and bring some money back for the Green Ranch. It was as if nothing had ever happened at the corrals with Dan Slayter.

"Now can you see what I'm telling you about Ben Hutton?" Lucy said to her mother after she got off the phone. "We can't depend on him. We're going to have to hire some hands to help us, there is no way around it."

Lucy went back to the table and sat with her mother to discuss the future of the Green Ranch. It was mid-afternoon and Lucy had just dressed to ride her palomino around the barrels for a while.

While she talked with her mother, Lucy had her mind on what was going to happen if they didn't have help in watching the ranch. It was obvious to both of them that they could not watch the Canyon Mountain pasture by themselves and take care of things down at the ranch at the same time.

There was one bull left up on Canyon Mountain and both Martha and Lucy were certain that Big Jed Barlow would come after that one as well sooner or later.

"Wait for Ben to come back," Martha said. "He can help you hire some men. Though we can't afford it."

"Mother, I know we can't afford it," Lucy said. "I know the money is real tight. But if we lose that last bull, we haven't got a chance of saving this place."

Martha finally nodded. "I guess you're right. I don't know how we're going to make this work, not and keep all the payments up, but we'll have to figure out something."

Lucy had been thinking about her palomino and how well the horse was coming along racing around barrels. Lucy's previous success was encouraging and she knew that with the increasing interest in women's participation in rodeo, she could win some big purses.

"Maybe I can win enough money with Lady to help out some," Lucy suggested. "I think I can get her to run barrels faster than most any horse I know of."

"Lucy, that's dangerous," Martha said. "Besides, you're talking about going off to rodeos and you just got through saying Ben should be here and not running off on his own."

"I *make* money at rodeos, Mother," Lucy pointed out. "Ben loses everything he puts into it."

"I still wish you would stay here and give Ben a chance."

Lucy shook her head. "We can't depend on Ben. We have to depend on one another."

"You're really serious, aren't you?" Martha said. "You know I want you here. Why do you insist?"

Lucy took a deep breath. "Mother, you're going to have to come to the realization that Dad is gone. We've got to make it on our own now. I know I can make money on Lady. So why shouldn't I do it?"

"But it will be such a burden on you." Martha said. "Traveling all over like that. Then coming back here to help and watch the Canyon Mountain pasture."

"That's where the hands will come in," Lucy said. "We can hire them to watch the pasture for us, at least until we get ahead a little bit with the money end of things."

Martha poured more coffee for both of them and took a deep breath.

"If that's what you want to do, Lucy, then you go ahead and do it," she finally said. "I think you'll find it pretty hard to keep up both ends, but I imagine you'll do it."

"Of course I will," Lucy said. She was getting ready to go out to the corrals, working on putting her hair into a long pony tail behind her. Then she went to pulling her riding boots on.

"How do you intend to go about hiring hands?" Martha wanted to know.

"I'll ask Dan Slayter if he can give me some

recommendations," Lucy answered. "He knows a lot of the ranchers in the valley and he probably has a good idea who needs work and who would be best for us."

"That is a good idea," Martha said. "I know for a fact that Dan Slayter has our best interests at heart. But I can see one problem clearly, and that is, what if no one wants to work for us?"

Lucy looked up from pulling her boots on. "Why wouldn't anybody want to work for us?"

"Think about it," Martha said. "If Big Jed Barlow wants our ranch, he won't want anybody in the valley going to work for us to help us save it. Barlow packs a lot of weight and he might influence the good hands away from us."

Lucy straightened the tops down over her boots. She put her vest on over her blouse and made sure her hair was free from the collar in the back.

"One thing you have to remember, Mother," Lucy finally said. "Big Jed Barlow might pack a lot of weight in this valley, but he's not going to intimidate the better hands. I'm going to tell Dan Slayter I want the best hands this valley has to offer and I don't want to have to worry about what they think about Big Jed Barlow and the Cross Twelve Ranch. Whether Jed Barlow knows it or not, we're here to stay."

Lucy went out to the corrals and Martha watched for a time from the kitchen window. She thought about how hard it would be if they had to pack up and leave the ranch, and she kept looking down the road, hoping to see

Ben Hutton's pickup coming up the driveway.

But then she remembered that Ben was off on the rodeo circuit again, getting money to help them. She wondered why Lucy disliked him so and thought to herself that Lucy must have taken a liking to that young sheriff, Dan Slayter. Then she sat down in her chair in the living room and gazed at the wall, wondering if Dan Slayter wouldn't be a good man for Lucy.

Dan sat in the living room of his log cabin at the edge of town, catching up on his reading. He wore a faded pair of denims and a T-shirt that read, "If you love something, set it free; if it doesn't return to you, hunt it down with a .44 Magnum from Jack's Gun Shop."

Dan heard the doorbell and put the magazine aside. He was surprised to see Lucy Green standing on the doorstep, holding a box of chocolates in her hands.

"I do hate to bother you when you're off duty, Sheriff Slayter," she said. "Please accept this gift as a token of my appreciation for your time."

Dan was immediately surprised, but did a good job of hiding it.

"Think nothing of it," he said, letting her in and accepting the chocolates. "And you can call me Dan. Are there any dark chocolates in here?"

"I wouldn't do that to you," Lucy said.

"That makes me feel good," Dan said. "Can I offer you something — a drink or some iced tea? I have some soft drinks."

"I would like a shot of Irish cream in coffee, if you don't mind," Lucy said.

"I'll see what I can do," Dan told her.

Dan opened the door to the deck and let Lucy walk out and take a deck chair, where she gazed up into the broad sky overhead. The kitchen nook was next to the deck and he conversed with her while he prepared the coffee. The cool air was a welcome change from the heat of mid-day and the sounds of crickets and night birds was soothing to the soul.

"It's such a beautiful night," Lucy said. "I just wish things were better so that I could enjoy it."

"What would Ben think of you coming to talk to me like this?" Dan asked Lucy.

"To hell with Ben," she said. "He's off chasing a dream he'll never realize. I wanted him to stay and help Mother and me, but he thinks he knows better."

"When's your wedding?" Dan asked, coming out onto the deck with Lucy's coffee and Irish cream. He handed the cup to her and took a chair himself.

Lucy took the coffee and thanked Dan. "I'm not setting any dates for a wedding. Not for a while. Maybe not for a long while. A lot of things have changed. And I don't mean just between Ben and me."

"Your father is gone now and that's that," Dan said. "You have your life to live."

"Yes, you're right," Lucy said with a nod. "I

realize all that, but it still angers me how he had to die. He wasn't an old man by any means."

Dan sipped on his own coffee and pointed out a falling star that plummeted down through the darkness.

"That means good luck, you know," Dan said.

"You're doing your best to cheer me up, aren't you," Lucy said.

"I'm trying," Dan said.

"I don't know if you realize what kind of trouble my mother and I are in," Lucy told Dan. "We are going to have a hard time keeping our ranch, especially now that Big Jed Barlow has managed to rustle another one of our prize bulls. We can't afford to lose the last one."

"I'm working on the evidence we have," Dan said. "But the evidence points to one of the hands and not to Barlow himself. And the hand has apparently skipped the county. That's makes it difficult to put any pressure on Barlow himself."

"What kind of evidence do you have?" Lucy asked.

Dan thought about whether or not he should discuss official business with Lucy, but he decided that she could be valuable in helping him watch for Brice Foster when he returned to the Cross 12 to resume working for Big Jed Barlow. It was certain Barlow wouldn't make another move toward stealing the last remaining bull or any of the Green Ranch cattle until Foster was back. With Lucy and her mother right next door, Lucy could possibly be watching for Foster's return.

"We found a little vial that contained the anesthesia used in drugging the bull they stole," Dan said. "That little vial had fingerprints on it belonging to a man named Brice Foster. Have you ever heard of him?"

"No, but I'm sure Mother has," Lucy said. "She and my dad were making a list of every hand who worked for Barlow."

"Why didn't you tell me this before?" Dan asked. "I could use that list."

"I'll get a copy to you," Lucy said. "I'm sure all the hands Big Jed Barlow has working for him are experts at stealing other people's livestock. He wouldn't hire anyone who wasn't a sworn outlaw."

"Sooner or later Foster is going to show up around here again to try and get your last bull," Dan said. "Someone like Foster can't stay away from that kind of money. When he comes back, I'll get him. Then we'll see what he has to say about Big Jed Barlow and his brother, Chet. Foster won't want to go to jail all by himself."

Dan noticed Lucy was thinking all the time. She had a lot to be concerned about. To Dan she seemed distant, but not shy. She was the kind of woman who either liked you—and liked you a lot—or didn't bother to give you the time of day.

Lucy was still wondering who this man, Dan Slayter, truly was. She had yet to really show how she felt about him. He was certainly a lot more interesting than Ben. She was beginning to wonder what it was she had ever seen in him.

Lucy Green had seen a lot of life already. She

had learned a lot ever before deciding to go to college. Growing up an only child had bestowed upon her an equal number of advantages and disadvantages. As far as men were concerned, she could take them or leave them. She saw Dan Slayter as somewhat of a challenge, as he didn't seem to be particularly overpowered by her beauty. But she was still going to be reserved around him.

"I know you plan to do the best you can for my mother and myself," Lucy finally said. "But we're going to need some outside help as well. I was hoping you might be able to recommend some people we could hire as cowhands—good men not easily intimidated."

"I'll have to give that some thought," Dan said. "I know your concern for getting the work done on your ranch, yet having enough money left over to pay the bills. I think you already know the men I will recommend will not be a bunch of vigilantes."

"That's why I came to you," Lucy said. "I'm serious about helping Mother keep the ranch, yet I don't intend to get into anything that will jeopardize us. Big Jed Barlow is good at getting away with murder. But I'm not going to try it."

"What about Ben Hutton?" Dan asked.

"That's the second time you've asked me about him," Lucy said. "The first time concerned a wedding, and I told you there wasn't going to be a wedding. Now I'm telling you there won't be a stock detective working for us. You told Mother and I that you could handle it. I believe you."

Dan asked Lucy if she cared for another cup of coffee and Irish cream. She declined. She got up from her chair and told him she had to be getting on back to the ranch, that her mother would be worried about her.

"After being away to college and on your own for as long as you have been, I doubt if your mother is too worried," Dan said.

Lucy smiled. "Maybe she's worried about my being with the sheriff of the county. Who knows what might happen."

"But you'll sure as hell be safe, won't you?" Dan said. "Sheriffs are known to keep beautiful ladies safe from harm."

Again Lucy wondered at Dan's attitude. She was standing next to him, enjoying what she was feeling from him. And she knew what he was feeling from her. Yet he was not coming on strong toward her as most men did in similar situations.

"Do you have a lady friend?" Lucy finally asked.

"Not me," Dan said with a smile. "I know some ladies who are my friends, but none who can claim to own me."

Lucy nodded. "I can see that it would be difficult to own you."

"Impossible," Dan said.

Lucy laughed. "Very well, then. Impossible. So what does it take to make you interested in a lady?"

"That depends entirely on the lady," Dan said. "And I know if I got interested in you, it would lead to big trouble."

"And how's that?" Lucy asked. Her voice had hardened a bit.

"Because it could get in between your mother and the case I'm building against the Cross Twelve Ranch. If you and I got to know one another and the word got out, then Big Jed Barlow could say I'm picking on him because I'm seeing you. Does that make sense?"

"You don't seem like a man who worries about what people think of you," Lucy said. "Why should Big Jed Barlow have that kind of influence?"

"In cases like this, anyone would have that kind of influence—whether or not he was Big Jed Barlow," Dan said.

Lucy nodded. "Well, maybe you're right. I don't know."

"Why don't we see what happens after I get Big Jed Barlow behind bars for good," Dan said. "Then maybe you and I could get to know one another better."

Lucy started down from the deck toward the pickup. Dan could tell she was insulted by what he had just told her. But he could see no other way, and she hadn't listened when he had told her he did like her.

"I don't want you to be mad at me," Dan called after Lucy. "I was just saying we should be careful for now. I would like to take you out later, when this is all settled."

Lucy was at the bottom of the steps. She turned

to Dan and he could see the frown on her face in the dim light.

"Don't hold your breath," she said. "By the time Big Jed Barlow is behind bars, it might be too late for you and me. Way too late."

Chapter Ten

"Now that Ben has left, do you think Sheriff Slayter will be the one for you?" Martha said to Lucy the next morning at breakfast. "I was thinking, he is a nice man, and he is sure of himself. He would be a good catch."

Lucy was forking through her bacon and eggs. She looked up at her mother with sudden surprise.

"I can't believe this, Mother. First you think Ben Hutton is just right, and now Dan Slayter. Who's next?"

Martha didn't feel much like eating herself. She toyed with her food while she mulled over what Lucy had just told her. It would be so nice if Lucy would settle down with a good man, a man who knew cows and horses and how to operate a ranch. Or at least someone who could help with the ranch.

"You've known so many men, Lucy," Martha finally said. "When do you think you're going to find the right one?"

Lucy jumped up from the table and threw her napkin down. "Thanks a lot, Mother! I know just what you're saying." She stomped from the table and across the kitchen toward the front door.

"Lucy, wait a minute," Martha said. She got up and followed her daughter. "You misunderstood me, Lucy. Just wait a minute, will you?"

Lucy was on her way to the barn and she wasn't slowing down. Martha began to run to catch up. Then she stopped and clutched at her chest. Lucy turned and saw what was happening and rushed back.

"Mother, take deep breaths," she said. "Just take deep breaths."

Lucy helped her mother back into the house, feeling guilty for having caused a problem. She felt angry at the same time, as her mother was tensed with resentment, almost resisting the help Lucy was offering.

"All right then, Mother," Lucy said when they got to the kitchen, "you just be angry with me. Because I'm certainly angry with you."

Martha was sitting at the table again, while Lucy was pacing the floor like a caged cat. Martha had managed to get some oxygen into her blood-stream by breathing deeply and was beginning to feel stronger as her heartbeat climbed. Her anger was evident as well.

"Lucy, I can't even talk to you anymore," she said. "I'm just disappointed that you and Ben are not getting along. That's all I said."

"That's not all you said," Lucy corrected her. "You also told me that I've had so many men I don't know which is which. Do you think I'm a whore? Is that really what you think?"

"Sit down for a minute, Lucy," Martha said. "You're driving me crazy marching around like that."

Lucy took a deep breath and plopped down into a chair next to her mother. The dishes were still on the table and Lucy moved them aside so she could put her elbows up and her chin in her hands.

"It's just that I can't understand you," Martha continued. "You seem so unsettled. Here you are nearly thirty years old and you can't make up your mind about your life."

"That's where you're wrong," Lucy quickly corrected her. She sat up in her chair and faced her mother directly. "I can and have made up my mind about my life. I'm going to live it the way *I* want to, not anybody else. I finally know who I am and I'm tired of trying to please everybody else. It's my turn to make the decisions for myself."

"What do you mean by that?" Martha asked.

"I mean, I should be able to decide who I want to marry and why. I don't think anybody else but me really knows who is best for me."

"What is wrong with Ben?"

"Mother, will you listen to me?" Lucy said, exasperated. "I'm not going to be like you and my father were, just sitting around pretending that life was fine. Maybe you stayed together because of me, or maybe because people your age just don't break up. I don't know. But I don't want to be that way."

Lucy could see her mother's face darken immediately.

"Lucy, what a thing to say!" Martha almost spat the words.

"Be real, Mother," Lucy said, even more angered. "It's time we be honest. It's time we talked about things that were never talked about before. I know you loved Dad a lot, but you had trouble understanding one another. You lived a life of hell with him. You put up with a lot from him, and he put up with a lot from you. I just don't want to have to go through that with the man I choose to spend my life with."

Lucy watched her mother's eyes and saw how they couldn't hide what was behind them—the hurt and anger of a lot of years with a man she had loved so much, yet couldn't understand at all. To Martha Green this was at the same time a moment of relief and one of intense vulnerability. Somehow her daughter had looked deep into her soul and had emptied it out.

Lucy took her mother into her arms as the tears spouted like water from a sudden spring. Lucy felt her own emotions flowing out now, releasing from all those years of knowing her parents were together, yet so far apart. It was out in the open and she wanted her mother to know that she held nothing against her, nothing at all. That was the way her life had been lived. It was past and they had the future to look forward to, a hard future at that.

Martha finally blew her nose into a tissue and for the first time since her husband's death on Canyon Mountain, she smiled.

"I guess I should give you credit for knowing all about your father and me," she told Lucy.

"You're no different than anybody else in this valley," Lucy said. "I'm no different than anybody else my age, either. We all have the same problems. They just wouldn't be as bad if we could face them and get them out."

Martha nodded. "You're right. But security to me has always been knowing just what was going to happen next. Your father and I lived knowing that the calves would come in the spring and we would sell them in the fall. Then we would feed hay over the winter and turn them out to graze once the snow left. I got so used to that."

"But you never knew how many calves you could save, nor how much they would sell for in the fall," Lucy pointed out. "And you never knew if it was going to be a good grass year or a poor grass year. You see, you never really knew what was going to happen next. There are no guarantees."

"Your father and I knew we both wanted the same things," Martha said. "We liked the life out here on the ranch and though we had our differences, we shared that feeling of being out in the open. But I must admit, I hated the feeling of being placed in a barrel with all the other women—everybody thinking that since we all were ranch wives, we were all the same."

"Think about it," Lucy said. "Everybody feels they have to follow everybody else and do whatever everybody else is doing—that they have to fit some mold of some kind. Well, that's not the way I look at it."

Martha was shaking her head. "No, Lucy, that's never the way you looked at it. I could never understand you."

"I just want to be free to be myself," Lucy said. "I watch the hawks and eagles fly over Canyon Mountain and I realize that even though they all fly in the sky and hunt the same way, each one of them is different from the other. They aren't concerned about what the other hawks and eagles think about them. I'm not either. I love this ranch and I love you. But I want to live my life the way I see fit."

"I've never wanted anything different for you," Martha said. "And you know your father wanted the best for you while he was alive."

"Your intentions are good, Mother, don't get me wrong," Lucy said. "But worrying about whether or not I will marry Ben Hutton or anybody else is telling me that you think I should live the same life you did. I can't do that."

Martha nodded. "I realize that, Lucy. I guess I've always known that."

"But you were just worried about what people would think because I'm different. Right? You wanted to prove to everybody in the valley that I'm not different."

Martha nodded again. "Yes, that's true."

"Please understand that I may never get married," Lucy then told her mother. "Sure, I've known a lot of men. And I've wished I could find one who really knew me. But just like Ben Hutton, none of them have been right for me. Maybe I don't have very good taste in men."

"What about that young sheriff?" Martha asked. "Does he have anything to do with your suddenly becoming bored with Ben Hutton."

Lucy shook her head, as if she was about to give up trying to get her point across to her mother. Finally she took a deep breath.

"Mother, Dan Slayter is the kind of man a lot of women would want," she said. "He's strong and good-looking and he doesn't look down on women. He's one of the few men I've met who doesn't feel intimidated by women in some way or another. But nobody's going to get Dan Slayter, and I'm certainly not going to try."

"Why do you let him get in the way of you and Ben?" Martha asked.

Lucy smiled. She realized her mother wasn't going to quit until she understood completely why Ben Hutton was no longer anybody special. And why if she didn't want Ben, she wouldn't go after Dan Slayter.

"I have to be honest with you, Mother," Lucy said. "Dan Slayter showed me that there really are men out there who are right for me. If Dan Slayter is one of them, then there have to be others like him. Meeting Dan just proved to me that Ben Hutton is not the one I want to marry."

Martha was silent for a time. She stared out the open door toward the corrals and beyond, where Canyon Mountain rose up into the summer sky. A lot had happened right here at the table in a short time, a lot of years had been brought out of the closet. It made her feel relieved in a way. But it also made her anxious. She knew that she was never going to influence Lucy in any way. She had to let Lucy live her own life the way she saw fit.

Finally Martha took a deep breath and turned back toward Lucy.

"I guess I can understand your feelings, Lucy," she said. "But it would sure be nice if you could find this man 'just like Dan Slayter' before too awful long. I need help here on this ranch."

"Why do we have to have a man to run it with us?" Lucy asked. "What's wrong with you and I running it?"

"It's hard," Martha said. "It's oh, so hard to try and keep things going without a husband."

Lucy could see how lost her mother was now without her father. It was such a dramatic change and suddenly there was a lot of pressure added to the loss — pressure in the form of aggression from Big Jed Barlow and the Cross 12 Ranch. Barlow could sense that the time was right to move in for the kill. And he was going to be moving fast now.

"I think we can take care of things just fine with the ranch hands helping us," Lucy said. "Dan Slayter knows the men who can help us. He wouldn't send us hands who felt awkward working for two women."

"So you think things will work out?" Martha asked.

"I know they will," Lucy said firmly. "You have to believe like me that they will."

Lucy knew it was important now to keep things as even as possible on a day-to-day basis. If things didn't level out, her mother's heart wasn't going to be able to hold out. Big Jed Barlow wasn't going to wait around to try and put the Green Ranch under so he could take control.

There was no question in Lucy's mind that her mother thought they needed Ben Hutton to help them against Big Jed Barlow. That was the main reason why she wanted Lucy to get serious with Ben Hutton. Now Lucy knew she was walking a fine line between choosing between her own happiness and keeping her mother alive.

The more Lucy thought about it, the more she realized that she would be of little help to her mother and little good to herself if she allowed the pressure to marry Ben Hutton weigh down her instincts. She decided that she was going to have to make her mother understand that her own life required that she be fulfilled by the right man — when and if he ever came along.

"If Ben comes back from the rodeo with money, what are you going to tell him?" Martha asked Lucy.

"I think we should forget about Ben Hutton and think about the hands we are hiring and how we can keep this ranch," Lucy said. "I have tried to tell you that I don't think Ben Hutton will come back. And if he does, I don't think he could help us against Big Jed Barlow anyway. If he could, he would be here now and not off eating arena dirt at some rodeo."

116

Martha got up from the table and started to clear it. Lucy knew she was thinking, possibly weighing in her own mind whether or not Ben Hutton could be an asset against Big Jed Barlow.

After a few minutes, Martha Green began to speak again.

"If Ben comes back and wants to help us," she told Lucy, "I think we ought to let him."

Lucy stopped drying the plate and stared at her mother. "I told you, I'm no longer interested in that man."

"That's not what I said," Martha told Lucy. "He can help us and still not be involved with you."

Lucy thought a moment. Now her mother was coming up with the very idea she had tried not long before. But Lucy wondered if her mother wasn't hoping she would come to care for Ben Hutton, if Hutton came back and stayed on.

Lucy knew that Hutton wanted her as well as the ranch and that he didn't want to be a hired hand. She decided her mother would have to find that out for herself.

"If you want Ben Hutton back, you tell him," Lucy said. "I don't want to have to get into it with him again."

"I'll tell him," Martha said with a nod.

Lucy stepped outside the house and looked into the morning sky. She felt alone, as if there was no one but herself who could understand the problems she was facing. Her mother seemed insistent they depend on Ben Hutton for help, when it was plain that Ben Hutton couldn't even help himself.

Lucy knew the reason her mother had gone back to hoping she would get to liking Ben Hutton again. It was the fact that Dan Slayter was a lawman and as such would not be a good choice for a husband. There was no question Dan Slayter could provide for her, but his work was dangerous. And he couldn't help as much on the ranch.

Despite the fact that she still was angry at Dan, Lucy made herself realize that what he had told her the night before was true. If he started taking her out, it would be bad for both of them. She knew he liked her, but she also knew he was smart and practical. Maybe he would want to see her when all of this was over.

Lucy realized that getting this all over should be her main concern now. It was plain to her that she would just have to take things into her own hands. She was going to have to see to it that they hired some men to help — the right men — so that she could make some money riding Lady in barrel races at the rodeos. The extra money was important.

And she was going to have to watch over her mother as well as the ranch. Both her mother and the ranch were very vulnerable right now. She didn't want to lose either of them.

Chapter Eleven

Nearly a week passed before Lucy called in to apologize for her behavior at Dan's cabin. She asked him to help her hire some men to work for them. The summer rodeo season was now in full swing and she was having trouble deciding whether to stay at the ranch or leave to make money. She knew she had to go and make what money she could, but she needed hands to be there and watch the Canyon Mountain pasture while she was gone.

Dan began to check around for men who might want to work for Lucy and Martha Green. He found it a more difficult task than he had expected. No one seemed available, though it appeared there were any number of cowhands out of work. Dan realized that the word had gotten around that Big Jed Barlow and his hands would come down hard on anyone working for the Green Ranch.

That eliminated most of the men who did not care for trouble. But there were a few men who showed up primarily because they had a score to settle with Big Jed Barlow and the Cross 12 Ranch.

Three men who had been former hands for the Cross 12 wanted work at the Green Ranch. These hands disliked the Cross 12 band, for they had left Big Jed Barlow under bitter circumstances. When they heard the news that the Green Ranch was hiring, they offered their services immediately. And they said they knew where they might be able to get more men.

Lucy made another call to Dan from the Green Ranch early one morning, just as he was settling into a new day at the office. He didn't expect what he heard.

"I want to thank you for the men you sent me, Dan," she said. "I have five good hands here now, all who look to me like they could ride for Pancho Villa. They are just what I need. Where did you find them?"

"I'll tell you the truth," Dan said. "I didn't find you any suitable hands. I heard there were some men who had once worked for the Cross Twelve who wanted to side with somebody else against him. But I sure didn't send them to you."

"It doesn't matter," Lucy said. "I now have the hands I need."

"Are they cowhands or gunhands?" Dan asked her.

"Probably both," Lucy answered.

"I was trying to get good cowhands," Dan said. "But the word is out that Big Jed Barlow has declared war on the Green Ranch."

"I would like to tell Big Jed Barlow that he has things wrong," Lucy said. "He should know that the Green Ranch has declared war on the Cross

120

Twelve, not the other way around."

"I don't like to hear any of it," Dan said. "None of this fits into the right side of the law."

"I can't help it," Lucy told him. "I've got to help my mother and keep this ranch operating. If Barlow thinks he's going to get the Green Ranch, he's sadly mistaken."

"How about Ben Hutton?" Dan asked. "Has he come back yet?"

"He's still on the rodeo circuit, as far as I know," Lucy said. "I really don't know for sure. He called once, three days after he left, but I haven't seen or heard from him since."

"What are you going to do about the men who want to work for you?" Dan asked.

"I think I'll hire them," Lucy said. "They realize they won't get much. But they sure do want a chance at Barlow. They'll guard the Canyon Mountain pasture well, I think."

Lucy told Dan that she was going up to the Three Forks rodeo to see if she couldn't win some money on her palomino. She asked Dan if he wanted to come and watch her but he declined politely. There was no way he was going to leave Clark County, not with Big Jed Barlow showing his anger.

"You didn't give those hands permission to start shooting whoever they want, I hope," Dan said to Lucy.

"I just told them they were to keep the Canyon Mountain pasture free of rustlers," Lucy said. "That's their job. How they do it is up to them."

"Lucy, I don't want you getting yourself into trouble," Dan said.

"I won't," Lucy told him. "I'm just going to a rodeo."

Dan wished Lucy good luck and hung up the phone. He thought about taking some deputies up on Canyon Mountain and staking it out. But that would cost a lot of money and there was no guarantee that they would do any good. The hands Lucy had hired certainly wouldn't be causing trouble, and Big Jed Barlow was smarter than to try and rustle cattle when he knew full well the law was standing directly in his way.

Barlow would wait until the right time to do his rustling. Brice Foster was still not back in the county and Dan figured Barlow would wait until his right hand man had healed from his gunshot wound. Then there was no telling what would happen. But it was certain the range war that had started up on Canyon Mountain was going to get hotter.

Brice Foster had changed the brands on over twenty head of cattle in the three-week period he had been staying at the Diamond 6. He had earned some good money and he was itching to spend it.

Foster wasn't as concerned now about being recognized anywhere. He had grown a beard that hid his identity well enough. And the big ten-gallon Stetson he had taken to wearing came low enough over his eyes that he could make himself almost invisible to those around him.

For that reason he was determined not to let Big Jed Barlow tell him he couldn't go anywhere anymore. He wanted to be sure Barlow knew he intended to do as he pleased now. If he had to wait around until the time was right to finish the job on Canyon Mountain, he could at least be enjoying himself in the meantime.

Big Jed Barlow wasn't calling on a daily basis anymore—not since he thought Foster was settled in changing brands on stolen cattle. Foster enjoyed that as much as anything, since he and Big Jed Barlow had been growing ever more distant from one another. All Foster cared to do now was to change the brand on that last Green Ranch bull and get back down to Nevada.

He was long overdue on a job down there and there was no way he could get word to them of his delay. They were in a remote area where there were no phones and Foster hadn't told them where he was working up in Montana. Now he was risking losing additional money on another job.

Despite that fact, Foster knew his best bet was to stay with Big Jed Barlow and to finish the job on Canyon Mountain. There was a lot of money at stake in this deal—way more than any three other jobs combined—and he wasn't about to walk away from it.

But he still could not stand to be kept at one place for very long. That did something to him that overshadowed all good sense. It made him crazy in a way—made him determined to do whatever he wanted, despite the outcome.

His determination to do what he wanted came

just after a call from Big Jed Barlow, the first one in three days. Foster took the phone from one of the Diamond 6 hands. He heard Big Jed's voice at the other end of the line.

"Brice, I thought I'd give you some good news."

"Good news?" Foster said. "The only good news I can think of is that I'm headed back down to the Cross Twelve to finish up what I started there."

Big Jed chuckled. "You got it. Just three or four more days and we'll be up on Canyon Mountain."

"Three or four more days? I thought you were going to tell me the Diamond Six boys were going to bring me back down today."

"No, it will be about the middle of next week," Barlow corrected him. "Then we'll have you back down here."

Foster's anger began to rise. He couldn't understand what was keeping them from taking him down that day—or at least in the next few days. Then he remembered the Diamond 6 hands talking about the rodeo in Three Forks and how they wanted to be there. Foster wondered if the Cross 12 hands were thinking the same thing and Barlow was just putting the job off until after the weekend.

Foster cleared his throat. "Big Jed, you going to the Three Forks rodeo?"

There was a silence at the other end. Then Big Jed answered, "No, I've got a lot of things to do around here. I don't know why you ask."

"It seems to me that the rodeos are taking precedence over the important work around here," Foster said. "I can't understand that."

124

"I don't know what you mean," Barlow said.

"I think you know what I mean," Foster said. "The hands from both the Diamond Six up here and the Cross Twelve down there want to make that rodeo. I think they ought to be ready to finish the job on Canyon Mountain first."

"Look, Foster, rodeo or no rodeo, the time isn't right yet to hit Canyon Mountain." Barlow was now angry himself. "Lucy and Martha Green have hired some hands that are watching things pretty careful. We can't just go up there without a good plan."

"How long does it take to make a good plan?" Foster was wondering. "I've been here over three weeks. It seems to me that's long enough for a good plan. What the hell is going on?"

"Get something straight, Foster," Barlow said. "You're working for me. And as long as you do, you'll take my orders. You got that."

"Well, I'm tired of taking orders from you," Foster said.

"Have it your way," Barlow told him. "But you won't see a dime of that money you earned branding those Green Ranch bulls. Say goodbye to that."

Foster tried to calm himself. He had visions of shooting Big Jed Barlow between the eyes. But he realized that would be foolish until after he collected his money.

Then he began to wonder if he ever would collect his money. He thought about Barlow doublecrossing him and not paying him at all, even after he finished with the last Green Ranch bull. He began to think of ways to insure himself against that.

"I've got an idea about money," Foster finally told Barlow. "I'm not doing that last bull until you give me the money for the first three. You got that."

"If I give you that money, how am I to know you'll finish the last bull for me?" Barlow asked. "You might just take off. I need the brand changed on that last bull."

"That's fine," Foster said. "I just want to know everything will work out for both of us. You can pay me when I get there and I'll even take some of the hands with me to the bank. Then they can escort me back to the ranch. How does that sound?"

After a silence Barlow finally agreed that the terms would suit him. They ended the conversation with another argument over whether Foster could come down right away, or wait until after the weekend.

"I told you, I want you there until the last possible minute," Barlow emphasized. "Slayter will be looking for you, even yet. He hasn't forgotten you."

"I can stay away from him," Foster said. "I'm just tired of this hide and seek stuff up here."

"Just hang on until next week," Barlow told him. "Then it will be all over. See you then."

Barlow hung up the phone before Foster could say anything more. Foster immediately became angry again. He walked around the ranch yard for a time, thinking how he was being played a fool by

Big Jed. He thought more about it and decided it was a combination of Big Jed and his brother, Chet. There would never be any good feelings between himself and Chet.

Foster finally decided he wasn't going to listen to Big Jed Barlow. He had some money from changing brands for the Diamond 6 and he was itching to spend it.

Later that afternoon, he found a pickup in the yard with the keys in it. Most of the hands had already left for the rodeo in Three Forks and those still around were either lounging inside the main ranch house or somewhere else.

Foster saw his chance to get away and took it. He jumped into the pickup and drove off without causing a disturbance. Within a short time he was out along the gravel road, looking into the distance where the highway met at the bottom of the hill.

He laughed and shouted in the cab as he sped along between the fences, enjoying the scenery and thinking about the adventure that lay in store for him down the road at Three Forks. He was free to be his own man once again and he vowed to himself that no matter what, that would never change.

Chapter Twelve

Foster got as far as Helena and stopped at a bar on Last Chance Gulch. Three Forks could wait for a while. He wanted to be able to enjoy some night life for a change. This was something he wanted to get used to once again.

He went from one bar to another, just listening to talk other than what he had become used to most of the summer. It was refreshing for a change and it was relaxing to be someplace where nobody seemed to know you and there wasn't someone watching you from the corner of his eye every second.

The only complaint Foster had was the soreness in his gunshot wound. It was healed for the most part, but there was still some itching and aching, especially whenever he used his arms to any degree. Lifting beers fell into that category.

After four hours of drinking, Foster somehow managed to find the pickup and get inside. The next thing he remembered was the sun shining directly in his face, causing him to sweat. He drove out of town and found a little cafe in Townsend, then got into Three Forks shortly after noon.

The assembly of cowboys and horse trailers and banners strung up throughout the little town attracted Foster's attention. It was the first time he had really been anywhere on his own for two days in a row, since being shot up on Canyon Mountain by Jack Green. His newfound freedom was exploding within him and he decided that it was time he allowed himself the luxuries of once again being his own man.

Three Forks was alive with the festivities of the rodeo. There was a parade in progress and people lined the streets to watch all manner of horses and riders pass them, each dressed in riding habits from the past. Wagons passed as well and there was even a stagecoach that had been brought in from Virginia City for the occasion.

Foster watched it all. He eyed the women as they rode, or came and went along the streets. He hadn't been with one since getting shot and he felt it was time that he enjoyed something he had grown accustomed to being without. He had gotten too drunk the night before, but vowed to himself that wouldn't happen today.

But there was time for that later, Foster realized. It was too early in the day for women with the same thing on their minds to be out looking around. He would take in the rodeo and then he would find someone at one of the local bars.

Foster bought his ticket and found a place in the grandstands to sit. He scratched his beard now and then as he watched the events — the saddle and bareback bronc riding and a round of calf roping. He got up on occasion to buy beer, but otherwise he stayed where he was.

It made him nervous to observe that some of the Cross 12 cowhands were seated just below him and off to the right. They did not pay any attention to him, even though a few of them turned around to look through the crowd for people they knew. Foster kept his hat low and knew that his beard would do the rest to conceal him.

The more he thought about it, the more he realized he was acting crazy. Why should he feel like this about being out on his own? He had every right to be his own man. And there wasn't much chance anyone was going to recognize him now, not with the beard.

Foster began to think that it was just Big Jed Barlow. He was a man who demanded control of everything—even the people he worked with on just a short-time basis. Foster began to realize that even though Big Jed Barlow paid top money to his help, he demanded so much of them that it seldom was worth the extra cash.

After drinking for a time longer, Foster grew restless and decided it was time to start looking for a lady. During the barrel racing event of the rodeo, he spotted a woman who was riding a palomino horse in the competition. She rode well and it was obvious that her time was going to be the best of the afternoon. When she came out of the arena on her horse, Foster watched her closely.

She was the woman he decided he wanted. She

had a lot of red hair and was strikingly good looking. What was even more tempting about her was her name. He had been listening to the announcer during the competition and realized he was watching Lucy Green.

Foster smiled to himself. She wouldn't know him; she wouldn't have any way of knowing him. He felt he was reasonably good looking and could likely gain her affections, at least for one night. His odds might be better if he told her he was one of the rodeo riders.

Foster worked his way among the horse trailers to where Lucy was loading her palomino. It was obvious that she was getting ready to leave for home and Foster realized he would have to act fast.

"That was a real good ride, miss," Foster said, removing his hat.

Lucy turned from closing the back doors of her stock trailer. The voice startled her and she jumped. She turned around to see a man she didn't know standing close to her.

"Thank you," she said politely. "I've got a good horse and that's what makes the difference."

"Yes, but you ride well, too," Foster said. "Don't sell yourself short."

Lucy noticed the man was trying to keep her from moving around the trailer toward her pickup. She finally realized she was going to have to tell him that she had to get on the road and back to her ranch.

"I've got to be going now," Lucy finally said.

"It was nice talking to you."

"Don't be in such a rush," Foster said. "I thought maybe we'd have a beer someplace downtown."

"Not today," Lucy said. "Maybe some other time."

Lucy started for her pickup again and Foster stepped in front of her.

"Just one?" he said. "It can be a short one."

"No thank you," Lucy said again. She started to walk around him.

Foster looked around and could see that no one was paying particular attention; and since they were on the opposite side of the trailer from the roadway, no one was likely to come around the trailer and see them. Foster decided he would take advantage of the situation.

Lucy found herself pushed up against the horse trailer. Foster had put his arms around her shoulders, pinning her arms at her sides. He was trying to kiss her and he knocked her hat off pushing his mouth against hers.

Lucy struggled to get free, but he was holding her tightly. She yelled, hoping to attract attention. But Foster did not seem deterred in what he was doing. Finally, Lucy managed to step hard on Foster's instep with her boot and he released her.

While Foster was limping on one foot, Lucy took a rope from where it was hung inside the stock trailer and walked toward Foster. As he looked up at her in anger, she swung the rope as hard as she could.

132

Foster took the blow full in the face. He fell backward to the ground. He started to get up quickly to come at Lucy, but a crowd was starting to gather and he thought better of it.

"I don't know who you are, mister," Lucy told him. "But if you ever try that with me again, you may not be so lucky."

Lucy turned and hurried toward her pickup. She got in and drove away quickly, embarrassed at the situation and concerned that the man would know who she was and come looking for her. She drove out of the rodeo grounds and didn't slow down until she had gotten out of Three Forks toward the interstate.

Foster walked away from the crowd and held the side of his face. The rope had struck him solidly and there was a large red welt across the bridge of his nose. It carried across the left side of his face as well, but was masked by the beard. But the nose stood out and he knew he was going to be marked this way for a few days.

He cursed his luck and his stupidity. Now it would be impossible to get any women interested in him. Welts across the face don't make for appealing looks. He thought about just going on down the road to the Cross 12, but decided he would stop downtown for a beer before he left. Maybe there would be another time with Lucy Green.

Big Jed Barlow had just gotten off the phone

with the owner of the Diamond 6 Ranch. Brice Foster had stolen one of their pickups and was gone. No one knew where he was.

Big Jed was fit to be tied. Chet was out in the bunkhouse playing poker with the few hands who had not gone to Three Forks to the rodeo. Big Jed was getting ready to go out to the bunkhouse to get Chet and discuss the problem of Foster when the phone rang again.

It was the helicopter pilot, calling from Canada, and he was angry.

The pilot was wondering when he was supposed to come down to finish the job he had set up with Barlow. There had been quite a bit of time elapsed between rustling runs up on Canyon Mountain — and Big Jed Barlow owed him some money.

Barlow told him there had been some delays. The pilot was aware that Brice Foster had been wounded and that he had been sent into hiding until he could heal up. Barlow said that Foster was back to health again, but that complications with hired hands on the Green Ranch was making it hard to get back on top of Canyon Mountain without a fight. He wasn't about to say anything about Foster having run wild across the state somewhere, and that there was going to be an all-out search for him.

Instead Barlow tried to tell the pilot that things were looking up for a successful last run to Canyon Mountain to get the last Charolais bull from the Green Ranch. But nothing Big Jed Barlow said made the pilot feel any better. The pilot told Barlow he had waited long enough and that it seemed to him that enough time had gone by to accommodate everything.

"The longer we wait on this thing, the harder it's going to be to get it done right," the pilot was saying. "I don't like flying in and out of there any more than I have to, even if you pay good money each run. Helicopters flying around at night make people wonder."

"One last time is all you'll need to come," Barlow promised. "Just once more and everyone goes home rich."

"I've heard that before," the pilot said. "So far that's only a pipe dream. I'm asking you if there is going to be another run down there soon, or if I should be offering my services elsewhere?"

"It's not going to do you a lot of good to get anxious," Barlow said. "There'll be another run — soon — and you'll get your share of the money. Just be there. It could be any day now when I call you."

Barlow told the pilot he would sweeten the pot for him. But it didn't seem to quell his anger. Nothing could make him feel better but getting the job finished and getting the rest of his money out of the deal.

Barlow had no more than hung up the phone when Chet came in from the bunkhouse and told him a couple of the hands had returned from Three Forks for some things and had been talking about Brice Foster being there.

"What did you say?" Big Jed asked him. "Brice Foster is at Three Forks?"

"It sounds like it to me," Chet answered. "Some of the hands were saying that a guy with a beard who was built like Foster was making a play for Lucy Green and she clubbed him across the face with a rope. If it was Foster, he ought to have a pretty sore nose."

"It's bad enough that he gets crazy and runs off in a Diamond Six pickup," Big Jed said, "but now he's going after Lucy Green. Doesn't he have a brain in his head?"

"Who were you on the phone with?" Chet asked. "It didn't seem to me that you were too happy when I came in."

"The pilot is about to quit us," Big Jed told him. "He's afraid if we wait too long, somebody will get onto him and he'll have trouble once he gets down here."

"Smart man," Chet observed. "Does he know about Foster?"

Big Jed shook his head. "No, or he wouldn't even consider coming down again. We've got to get this job finished. Now!"

"What about Foster?" Chet wondered.

"We'd better go to Three Forks and see if we can find him," Big Jed told Chet. "We'd better get there before Foster gets himself in real trouble and pulls us down with him."

Chapter Thirteen

Ben Hutton didn't care to even finish the second round of the saddle bronc competition. He had been thrown during the bareback ride and he had sprained his ankle badly. Most all of the cowboys rode with injuries, but Hutton was more concerned about seeing if he could find Lucy Green.

Hutton limped around the rodeo grounds for a time, asking if anyone had seen Lucy. He finally learned that she had gone back to Clark City. It had been some time back when she left, and it was said she had been fighting with some man she had struck with a rope.

Hutton felt anger and depression setting in. Lucy had promised to talk to him here and now she was gone. And the way it sounded, she had had some kind of lover's quarrel with someone. He wondered if she was seeing somebody and what he could do to get between them.

If anybody could help him it would be Lucy's mother, Martha. For some reason that woman thought more of him than anyone ever had. Hutton realized Martha really didn't know him all that well and it seemed as if she was just anxious for Lucy to settle down. He wished Lucy would take her advice.

Hutton saw no reason to go back to Clark City right away. It would take him some time before he could decide what he wanted to say to Lucy once he did see her again. It was going to be almost impossible now to get her back.

He found a bar downtown to drown his sorrows in and drank two beers in less than five minutes. Then he went to the pool table and challenged anyone in the house to five dollars a game. He realized he couldn't rodeo, but pool was one game he was better at than most.

There were a number of cowboys from the rodeo circuit in the bar and one of them stepped up right away. Hutton racked the balls and when the cowboy failed to get a ball on the break, Hutton ran the table.

The cowboy ended up losing fifteen dollars to Hutton before he quit. This made Hutton feel a lot better—it made him feel like he was the hero he had always wanted to be. The cowboy finally gave up and Foster looked around the room.

Two others in the bar tried him in turn and they both lost their money as well. When it seemed to Hutton as if he had conquered the bar, a cowboy in a beard and a big hat stepped forward and found himself a cue.

Brice Foster had been standing against the bar watching everything for some time. He had been staying off by himself, nursing his swollen face. Up until now he hadn't been interested in drawing attention to himself. But he was tired of seeing this blowhard cowboy beating just average competition.

It was Foster's nature to see just how good pool players were before he challenged them. He, too, was used to winning people's money. He put a ten dollar bill down and watched Ben Hutton's face turn to surprise.

"You sure you want to play for that much?" Hutton asked him.

"If you can stand to lose it," Foster said.

"I don't intend to lose," Hutton said.

Hutton chalked his cue and studied the cowboy who had challenged him while the cowboy racked the balls. Even though the cowboy was bearded and his big hat was pulled low over his eyes, he could see that the cowboy's nose was one big, red welt. He thought about it and concluded that this must be the cowboy who had made the play for Lucy.

"Did you ride today?" Hutton asked him.

Foster shook his head and put the rack away. He chalked his own cue and studied the money lying on the edge of the table.

"I don't ride the circuit," he said. "I wager my money only when I'm sure I'm going to come out ahead — way ahead."

"It doesn't appear that you came out ahead with Lucy Green," Hutton said.

Foster looked up at him quickly. "What did you say?"

"I just wanted to know if you knew Lucy Green. That's all."

The bar was quiet now. Everyone was watching what was going on. There were even more people coming in who had heard there was something happening that could be real interesting.

"What if I do know Lucy Green?" Foster asked. "What's that to you?"

"I'm going to marry her."

"That's not what she said when she was out with me last night."

Hutton stiffened immediately. Then he let down some, knowing this cowboy had just been thrashed across the face by Lucy and couldn't possibly want to do anything but get him off his pool game.

"It seems to me that Lucy had no intention of going out with you," Hutton said and chuckled. "At least, that's what your nose would seem to indicate."

"Maybe you would like a nose just like mine," Foster suggested.

Hutton noticed the cowboy was standing erect, challenging him directly. Hutton felt a fear creeping into his stomach. It was the same thing—he would get himself into a situation like this and have to figure a way out of it, or get himself beat up in a fight.

The way this cowboy looked, and the expression of anger that he held, indicated he would be a tough one in a fight. Hutton decided wisely to work his way out of it with words.

"I think you just want to avoid the pool game," Hutton finally said. "You're not so sure now if you want to lose your money."

"We'll see about that," Foster said. "Your

break."

Hutton broke but failed to get any ball to fall. Foster then ran the table. The crowd in the bar began to buzz; it appeared as if Ben Hutton had met his match.

But Hutton didn't miss any more shots that would put him in jeopardy of losing any games and he took thirty dollars from Foster in less than an hour. Foster's face was sore and his expression wasn't pleasant to begin with. But after losing for the sixth time, he began to glare at Hutton.

"This must be your lucky day," Foster said.

"Or your unlucky one," Hutton said. "Care to lose any more money?"

"I was thinking we could play for twenty a game now," Foster said. "How does that sound?"

Hutton straightened up and leaned against his cue. He studied Foster for a time and finally reached into his pocket.

"I don't think you can stand to lose any more of your money," Hutton said. "But if you insist."

Foster was stretching his twenty-dollar bill between his fingers when he noticed a group of men coming into the bar. Leading them was Big Jed Barlow, with his brother, Chet, and they were coming straight for the pool table.

Foster stood rigid. Chet stood back with the hands while Big Jed walked up to him and just glared down at him for a time. Finally, Big Jed took the twenty from Foster's hand and put it into Foster's shirt pocket.

"You haven't got time for all this," Barlow said in a low, hard drawl. "You're not even supposed to be here. It's time to leave."

Foster realized the entire bar was silent. Everyone was watching them. He had made a fool of himself going after Lucy Green at the rodeo and he had just lost good money here. Now Barlow was treating him like a schoolboy. He just lowered his hat down over his eyes and walked toward the door.

Once outside, Big Jed and Chet Barlow and the hands caught up with him.

"What the hell do you think you're doing?" Chet wanted to know. "You don't seem to care much about anything. Big Jed and I are trying to make us all a lot of money and you're intent on getting us all thrown in jail. What's the deal?"

Foster turned on Chet. He had his hands on his hips. The day had so far been way too long for him.

"Listen, I don't give a damn," Foster said. "I haven't been out on the town for a long time. I just wanted to do a little drinking, and maybe find a woman or something."

"Everything you needed was at the Diamond Six," Chet said. "And everything you needed is also at the Cross Twelve. You know that. Don't tell me you haven't had women or enough to drink since you've been working for us."

"That isn't it," Foster said. "I'm sick and tired of being nurse-maided. And if you and Big Jed think you can find somebody who can work on brands for you like I can, go find a telephone book."

Foster turned to walk away, but Big Jed grabbed him by the shirt and turned him around. The hands all surrounded him in a circle then.

"Just a damn minute!" Big Jed growled. "You're wanted for questioning by Dan Slayter. You know that, yet you're out here where everyone can see you. That doesn't make me very happy. Especially since you were working for me when you got shot. I thought we talked about that over the phone. You'd better get your head on straight."

"Nobody knows me," Foster argued. "Not with this beard."

"It seems to me that you want everybody to realize who you are," Big Jed told him. "Otherwise you wouldn't be doing what you are. Besides, some of the hands from the Cross Twelve who saw you get whacked by Lucy Green figured out who you were easy enough. There's bound to be others who know."

Foster thought about it for a moment. He could see that Big Jed was right. He could see where Barlow was providing him with everything he needed, yet he was taking chances going out among people and risking being recognized. It stood to reason that if some of the Cross 12 cowhands were at the rodeo and had seen him there, the law in the county might have just as easily figured out who he was. They could have told Dan Slayter.

"I'll go back to the Cross Twelve," Foster said. "I just wanted to do something on my own for a change."

"Wait until next week, Foster," Barlow said. "I told you that. The way you're going, you'll have us all in jail before the weekend is over. Now I'm

143

going to have to hide you out again. I don't like this."

"Why do you have to hide me out again?" Foster wanted to know.

Barlow leaned over and got closer to Foster's face. "Because when Slayter hears about this, he'll have every lawman between here and Canada notified. And the first thing he'll do is run your picture out again. See what I mean about being stupid?"

Foster shrugged. "I just wanted a little free time."

"I'm paying you good money to do what I say," Barlow told him. "After we get the last Green Ranch bull from Canyon Mountain, you're free to do whatever you please—because you won't be working for me anymore. Unless you want to quit now. Say one way or the other, so I'll know. I'm not sure you're worth all this."

Foster shrugged. "I'll stay on. Besides, you couldn't find anybody who could change brands as good as me."

Barlow grunted. "I'll have one of the hands take you to a cabin at the edge of the Beartooth Wilderness. Then you're going to stay at that cabin until I tell you to leave. Is that understood?"

Foster nodded. He didn't look Big Jed Barlow in the eye, but followed one of the hands to a pickup. He heard Barlow behind him telling him not to screw up again. Foster figured he could wait at the cabin at the edge of the Beartooth. It wouldn't be long until he could change the brand on that last Green Ranch bull and get back to Nevada. And he would never come back.

* * *

It was early evening and Dan was just getting ready to leave for home when Lucy Green came into the office. She was interested in seeing a picture of Brice Foster.

"I'm not sure," she told Dan, "but I think he was the man who made a pass at me over in Three Forks today."

Dan went to his desk, where he had a stack of information regarding the Cross 12 Ranch and the men who worked for Big Jed Barlow. He wanted to know the circumstances of Lucy's encounter with Foster—if it indeed was him—and why she thought it could be Foster. He was supposedly hiding out.

Lucy told Dan about the incident in Three Forks, describing a man with a beard, but with eyes that had made her wonder if she hadn't seen them somewhere before. The more she thought about it, the more she was sure she had seen them in a newspaper—one with Brice Foster's picture in it.

"He was close enough to me so that I could get a good look at his face," Lucy recalled with distaste. "He had a beard, but his eyes were what really caught my attention. I think he's crazy."

"There are a lot of people that way," Dan said, bringing up a black and white mug shot of Foster from the pile of material. "But Brice Foster is crazy in his own kind of way. Does that look like the man who bothered you?"

Lucy took the photo and studied it, looking

closely at the eyes. She was relatively sure it had been Foster. But she wanted to be positive.

"Are there any pictures of him with a beard?" she wanted to know.

"Let me work on that," Dan said. He found a felt marking pen in the drawer of his desk and quickly drew a beard on Brice Foster's face.

"No question," Lucy said. "That man was Brice Foster. I'm sure of it."

"Where did he go after you hit him with the rope?" Dan wanted to know.

"I have no idea. I really didn't care. I left without looking back, just because I wanted to get as far away from him as possible. That was crazy, what he tried in front of all those people. I still can't believe it."

"I'll get in touch with the authorities over there," Dan said. "Maybe they've gotten a report on that, or even something else that might have happened. A man as crazy as Foster is bound to cause trouble any number of places."

"I'm really afraid now," Lucy said. "I can see that they're going to be going up on Canyon Mountain any time now. They're going to want to finish the job they started."

"Lucy, I don't want you to panic now," Dan said. "If Foster is anywhere near, we'll find him and bring him in. I don't think Barlow will move on your pasture unless he has Foster to change the brand on your bull. It's real risky moving cattle without the proper papers."

"I don't think you know Big Jed Barlow," Lucy said. "He's apt to put up with just so much from

Foster and then try it on his own."

"Barlow knows better than to try and change brands on his own," Dan said. "That takes an expert."

"That's not what I mean," Lucy said. "Barlow wants us to go bankrupt so he can get the ranch from the bank. He also wants desperately to take the bull and sell him for the money. But if he thinks Foster isn't going to be able to help him any more, he may just decide he will get us off the ranch one way or the other—he may just go up on Canyon Mountain and shoot the bull."

Dan hadn't really thought much about that. Big Jed Barlow was a greedy man and if there was any way at all he could make fifty thousand dollars, he would do it. But if he was backed far enough into a corner, he might do what Lucy had just suggested.

"If he really wants our ranch badly enough," Lucy continued, "Barlow will use his head and just get rid of the bull. If it's dead, we can't use it and we're out the money. I think he's going to realize that soon."

Chapter Fourteen

Ben Hutton remained at the bar, getting over his surprise at seeing Big Jed Barlow — and Barlow's interaction with the cowboy he had been playing pool with. Though Hutton hadn't said anything at the time, he had wanted badly to confront Big Jed Barlow and his brother, Chet, as they talked to the cowboy whom he had beaten in pool. Hutton had wanted badly to slam the pool cue into Big Jed's head. But there had been no chance for that.

Hutton's surprise at seeing the Barlows was by now turning into anger. He hadn't forgotten how Big Jed had swindled him out of the prize Appaloosa stallion he had bought and traded to Barlow. The Barlows had been so intent on the cowboy that they hadn't even noticed him. But Hutton had noticed them and now it was time for payback.

As he leaned over the bar and finished a beer, Hutton thought about who the cowboy he had beaten in pool might be. He now realized that it had to be Brice Foster, the man wanted for questioning in the case of Jack Green's death.

Hutton now remembered seeing the picture of

Foster in the paper. But Foster had been without the beard at the time. Still, Hutton was sure the man had been Foster. Otherwise Big Jed Barlow wouldn't have been in such a hurry to usher him out of the bar.

And he wouldn't have been in such a hurry to get him into the blue Chevy pickup and out of town. Hutton had noticed that the pickup had River County plates—likely from the Cross 12 Ranch. He had made a note of the number on the plates. Now Hutton was certain he had been playing pool against Brice Foster. If only he had known while he was playing.

Hutton went to a pay phone and found a number for the Three Forks branch of the county sheriff's office. He dialed the number and told the dispatcher he wanted to speak to one of the officers on duty.

"I know where you can find Brice Foster," he said to the officer.

"The same Brice Foster who is wanted in River County?" the officer asked.

"The same," Hutton said. "He was here at the rodeo today, and now he's on his way back to River County."

Hutton then described the late model pickup and gave the license number. He declined to give his own name but told the officer he had been at the bar and had recognized Foster from a picture in the newspaper, even though Foster was now wearing a beard.

Hutton hung up the phone gloating. He would

go back to River County and to the Green Ranch and tell Lucy and her mother he had been instrumental in getting Brice Foster captured by the authorities. Then maybe Lucy would think of him as she should.

Brice Foster looked out into the late evening sky as he rode with the Cross 12 hand down the highway toward Clark City. It would be dark soon and the last bit of sunlight was dancing off the high peaks of the mountains that surrounded the valley through which they drove.

The Spanish Peaks seemed closer than they actually were, jutting up into the clear blue. There was the Bridger Range that rose to the north, climbing straight up off the valley floor into high rocks. And the Gallatin Range that worked its way around the south end of Bozeman, the town they were passing through, looked even bigger than usual in the clear evening air.

They got past Bozeman and worked their way up over the pass that led down into River County. Foster noticed how the rock walls faced both sides of the interstate just down over the pass. They reminded him of his three weeks of confinement, and the next few days that he would have to undergo before he could get away for good.

It was dark when they reached the River County line. Clark City was not far now. They intended to just get off the interstate at the second exit and go right into Paradise Valley, where the cabin was situated on a mountainside above Sixmile Creek.

As they traveled, Foster thought about getting the job done on Canyon Mountain and getting back down to Nevada. He didn't care as much now about the money—the incredibly good money Big Jed Barlow paid him for changing brands—but thought more about how much bad luck he had suffered since coming up. It was bad enough having been shot, but going crazy in seclusion was something he had never had to suffer through before.

It seemed ironic to Foster that the very rifle he had been shot with was resting on a gun rack across the back window. It was a re-tooled semi-automatic .30-06 that Jack Green had had with him on Canyon Mountain. Weller had played a series of poker hands with the other hands of the Cross 12 to see who would own the rifle. Big Jed Barlow hadn't wanted anything to do with the gun.

Now Foster couldn't help but think the rifle represented bad luck to him as well. He had been found by Big Jed Barlow playing pool in a Three Forks bar and was now on his way back to another secluded spot to await instructions about the rustling job on Canyon Mountain.

The hand he was riding with wasn't particularly talkative. He just drove and sometimes whistled. His name was Jim Weller. He was small and wiry, and dark complected, with shifty eyes that would move in his head to look at Foster and then go into a squint.

Foster didn't mind Weller squinting at him—he

was used to people doing that. In fact, most of the Cross 12 cowhands had squinted at him since the first day he arrived. He was getting paid much more than they were and each one of them wanted to know what was so special about him that made him such an expert at changing brands.

What made Foster nervous was the continuous silence. The drive seemed to take forever. Finally Weller squinted at Foster and told Foster that he had good taste in women—that almost anybody would risk getting whacked across the face with a rope for a chance at Lucy Green.

Foster didn't see any point in taking offense and threatening the hand; it wouldn't help his cause with Big Jed Barlow any and it certainly wouldn't speed up their trip. Foster only cared about getting to the cabin and waiting the few days until they went up on Canyon Mountain for the last time.

While they traveled, Foster did manage to get some information from Weller about where the cabin was located.

"Not far from Chico Hot Springs," Weller said with a smile on his face. "Lots of pretty ladies from all over go there to just sit in the water with not much on. If I was you, I might slip down there for a peek some time."

Foster's spirits raised immediately. He wouldn't be as isolated as he had first thought. In fact, he was beginning to get excited. There was no hot springs resort area near the Cross 12. It was just a bedraggled, spread-out ranch headquarters that brought boredom on almost as soon as you stepped foot on the property.

And the dogs—those two pit bull terriers—they were the only source of real activity around the place. No one else did much of anything but make sure the livestock were still within Cross 12 fence-lines. The dogs were the only things that moved much at all.

Big Jed had them trained into a frenzy, barking and lashing out at anything that wasn't part of the Cross 12. Big Jed didn't like visitors and the dogs were his security against anyone ever wanting to come back.

Foster was glad he wasn't going back to the Cross 12 to await the last trip up on Canyon Mountain. Though the cabin on Sixmile Creek would be isolated, the hand had talked about Chico not being far away. There would certainly be some fun to alleviate the boredom.

Foster was thinking about Chico when he noticed Dan Slayter's Jeep with the sheriff's star parked along the interstate. Weller noticed the Jeep at the same time and when both men looked back, the Jeep came out onto the interstate and the pursuit lights came on.

Foster cursed. "Get this thing moving!"

Weller was slowing down the pickup. "It ain't me they want. I'm getting out."

Foster pulled the .30-06 rifle off the back window and placed the barrel near Weller's ear.

"Not yet you're not. I said get this thing rolling!"

Weller stepped on the gas and the pickup sped

up. The Jeep was coming up quickly from behind, but Foster insisted they go faster.

"I can't make it go any faster!" Weller yelled. "Don't shoot me, I can't make it go faster."

"Slow down and pull off the roadway," Foster ordered.

Weller did what he was told and just before they came to a stop, Foster pulled the trigger on the .30-06. Weller jerked as the top of his head came off, spraying blood and brains and bone fragments all over the door and windshield, and blowing the window of the door out into small glass fragments.

The pickup started to veer toward the ditch and Foster dropped the rifle onto the floorboards. He took the steering wheel, noticing Dan Slayter's Jeep coming up fast now. Weller's body was slumped against the door.

Foster then cranked the handle of the door open and shoved Weller's lifeless body out onto the pavement in front of Dan Slayter's Jeep and sped off into the night. He didn't think about much of anything now but getting away from Slayter and finding his way to Chico Hot Springs.

Dan had been waiting with Leon along the interstate for nearly two hours, wondering if the report that Foster was headed back to River County was true. A report had come from Gallatin County and Dan had responded right away.

The last thing they had expected was to have the

154

hand driving the blue pickup take off at full speed. His pickup could not hope to outrun the Jeep in a chase. But when Leon pointed out that Foster had pulled a rifle from the gunrack along the back window, Dan realized the driver had no choice.

Now Dan was swerving to avoid the body of the driver as Foster pushed him out onto the roadway. Leon was yelling for him to look out; but it was too late to avoid hitting the body and Dan worked to keep the Jeep on four wheels as it bounced up over the rolling form and spun out for the ditch.

Dan got the Jeep under control as they went into the median between the two lanes of the interstate. A car coming up behind them swerved to miss the body and the driver of that vehicle lost control, sending it into a roll across the pavement.

Dan called for an ambulance and rushed across the road to assist whoever was in the car. It was a small sports car with a young man and a woman who appeared to be either his wife or his date with him. The woman had been thrown from the car and the man was pinned under the wreckage. Both were badly injured, but still breathing.

Leon stood beside Dan and they watched the tail lights of the blue pickup become lost in the distance. Dan was gritting his teeth.

"Can you handle this here, Leon?" he asked. "I can't see letting Brice Foster get away like that."

"You go ahead," Leon said. "I know what to do here."

Dan got back into his Jeep and started the engine. He called in his location again and asked the dispatcher to call the highway patrol for backup. Wherever Foster was headed, he would need some help in catching him.

Big Jed Barlow was again pacing the floor at the ranch house. He had been waiting for a long time for a phone call from Jim Weller. As soon as Foster was at the cabin, Weller was to have called to report in.

It was getting late and Big Jed was worried. Chet was telling him there was no doubt that Foster had gotten into trouble somehow. He was proved right when one of the hands came in from the bunkhouse to report that there was a special bulletin on the radio and television about a shooting and an accident on the interstate just outside of Clark City.

"They mentioned that it was Brice Foster who was suspected of the shooting," the hand said. "Did he kill Jim?"

Big Jed and Chet looked to one another. "Go back out to the bunkhouse," Big Jed told the hand. "And tell the others to get ready to move up on Canyon Mountain as soon as I give the order."

Big Jed went to the television set and turned it on. There was a commercial in progress, but the late news was about to begin.

"Now you're thinking smart," Chet told him. "Slayter is bound to be tied up in this affair and there won't be anybody to stop us from going up on the mountain."

While the newscaster talked about the shooting and the accident and the chase for Foster, Big Jed went to the phone and called the helicopter pilot in Canada. The pilot said he was on his way and Big Jed smiled.

"I think maybe we can get this done after all," he said.

Chapter Fifteen

Lucy drove into the yard just in time to see the hands all leaving for town. They waved as they drove past her and when she got into the house, she found her mother in the living room with Ben Hutton.

"Welcome back," Hutton said to her. "Congratulations on your win at Three Forks today."

"What are you doing here?" Lucy asked Hutton.

"Now, Lucy, be polite," Martha said. "Ben and I were just having a little talk, that's all."

"A little talk about what?"

"Ranch business," Martha said. "We were talking about ranch business."

Lucy looked hard at Hutton. She turned back to her mother. "I'm not sure I understand quite what you mean," she said.

"I'm going to join the hands in town now," Hutton said. "I'll leave you two alone."

"No need to rush off," Lucy said.

"I told the hands I would be with them," Hutton said. "They're already waiting for me now."

Hutton hurried out of the house and Lucy turned to her mother.

"I don't understand all this."

"I just put Ben in charge of the ranch. He's taking over the operations until we're sure Big Jed Barlow is no longer a threat to us."

Lucy stood speechless for a moment, staring at her mother. She was now even more confused than before. Her mother spoke again before she had a chance to recover.

"Ben told me that Dan Slayter knows where Brice Foster is and that Foster will soon be in jail. If that's the case, then maybe the Cross Twelve Ranch will back down."

"Mother, the Cross Twelve Ranch will never back down," Lucy said. "Big Jed Barlow is not built that way. He's going to come after us until he gets his way—either that or he's in his grave."

"Ben doesn't think so."

"Ben doesn't have the sense he was born with. And I can't believe you gave him control of this ranch, *our* ranch."

"Sometimes men make better decisions than women about what has to be done on a place," Martha said. "I think Ben has good potential and I just wanted him around to help us. He's been worried about how we were getting along and wanted to leave the rodeo circuit to help us. I think it was nice of him."

Lucy became so angry she could hardly talk. She tried to tell her mother that Ben Hutton was the last man on earth she should put in charge of anything. She walked to the picture window and watched as Hutton and the hands drove the last stretch of roadway in the distance, out toward the highway.

"Where is Hutton taking the hands?" she asked.

Martha smiled. "They're going to Chico for a little celebration. Since Brice Foster is likely headed for jail, Ben thought it might be nice to give the hands a night off."

"Don't you think the celebration is a bit premature?" Lucy asked. "Foster hasn't been captured yet and Big Jed Barlow and the rest of his hands aren't anywhere near a jail. I don't understand this—not at all."

"Lucy, just relax," Martha said. "That's what you're always telling me. Things are working out fine."

Lucy just about exploded. But she caught herself. She realized that she could get mad and then upset her mother to the point that her heart would act up. That wouldn't solve anything.

Instead, Lucy left the house and stomped out to the corrals. Her palomino was now well rested from the competition in Three Forks. Lucy went into the barn and gave the horse more oats. Then she took a deep breath.

"I don't know whether I'm going crazy or Mother is," Lucy said to her horse. "I'm afraid we both are. I just don't know what is going to happen next."

She talked to her palomino awhile longer and finally left the barn. Instead of returning to the house, she decided to take a walk up along the hillside behind the barn—just stroll the trail that went from the bottom up toward Canyon Mountain.

The night was still and the stars were out in thick clusters. Everything seemed calm and peaceful, but Lucy couldn't enjoy it. She worried about what could happen now that Ben Hutton was in charge of the hired hands, and if the ranch could even survive under those circumstances.

It made her wonder if her mother had completely lost her senses or if Ben Hutton had some kind of magic in his voice when it came to dealing with her mother. Hutton was nowhere near the man her father had been, yet Hutton seemed to promote himself so well that her mother was drawn to him.

As she walked, Lucy fought the urge to return to the house and ask her mother if she had decided Ben Hutton was more important to her than she was. But she knew it would only hurt her mother and cause more misunderstanding. Lucy knew she would never figure this all out.

As she thought, she heard a sound in the night — the sound of something in the air over Canyon Mountain. Lucy looked and saw the lights of some kind of craft and she knew instinctively that it was a helicopter.

Big Jed Barlow was planning a raid on the Canyon Mountain pasture.

Lucy turned on the trail. She began to trot in the darkness, and soon she was in a full run past the barn and corrals. When she burst into the house Martha was reading a magazine in the living room.

"Lucy, for heaven's sake, what's wrong?" she asked.

Lucy caught her breath. She was already at the telephone, dialing. "I just heard a helicopter over Canyon Mountain," she told her mother. "The Cross Twelve Ranch is making a run for the last bull. I've got to get hold of Dan."

"Lucy, he's out after Brice Foster," Martha reminded him.

Lucy talked to the dispatcher and told her what was happening. The dispatcher promised to try and get through to Dan by radio. Lucy then hung up the phone and turned to her mother.

"I'm going up there," she said. "I'm not going to let this happen without a fight."

"Lucy!" Martha said. "Please. Wait for Sheriff Slayter."

"I don't know how long that will be," Lucy said. She was at the gun cabinet, choosing one of her father's rifles. She picked up a box of cartridges and opened it.

"Why don't we wait for Ben?" Martha asked.

"I can't believe you're saying that," Lucy told her mother. "You just said they went to Chico to have fun. Hutton and the hands we hired won't do us any good now. I guess there's just me left."

Martha got up from her chair. "And there's me."

"Mother, you can't go," Lucy said.

"I can go, and I will go," Martha said. "I'm the one who let Ben take the hands to Chico. You can't stop me from going with you."

Lucy dialed the number at Chico Hot Springs

next. "I'm telling Ben Hutton to get back here," she said. "If he's working for us, he'll listen."

Lucy waited while the connection was made to the saloon. She waited, stepping from one foot to the other, stuffing cartridges from the box into her pockets. Finally, a voice at the other end said, "I'm sorry, Ben Hutton is not here."

Lucy hung up and picked up the rifle. She stopped at the door and watched her mother pull on a pair of boots.

"Don't you dare leave without me," Martha said.

"Mother, are you sure?" Lucy asked.

Martha Green came toward the door. "Let's go, Lucy," she said. "I've never been more sure of anything in my life."

Dan had followed Brice Foster up the old highway until he found the blue pickup abandoned a hundred yards from the turnoff that led to Chico Hot Springs. A motorist who had been run off the road told Dan it had been a blue pickup. He said he watched it turn off on the old highway that skirted the east side of the valley.

Dan hadn't seen the tail lights at all, even though he sped up the old highway and took the curves at a dangerous clip. He had been watching for Foster all the way and had radioed back to the office for help from the highway patrol, in case Foster made it back to the main highway.

Then Dan had found the pickup upon slowing

down at the corner where the road into Chico took off from the old highway. Now he was wondering where Foster would have gone, and why he had left the pickup where he did.

Upon examining it, Dan could see that the pickup had sustained a flat tire. Foster was gone and there was no way to tell which way he might have gone. Dan knew there was little chance he would catch Foster now—not in the middle of the night at the edge of the mountains.

Dan decided to see if Foster had for some reason stopped in the Chico Saloon. He went in to find a crowd of people enjoying a country band and whooping it up. Among those laughing and carrying on was Ben Hutton, along with the hands who had signed on to work for the Green Ranch.

Hutton sipped on a beer at the bar and ignored Dan until he made it plain to him he wanted to talk.

"This is official business, Hutton," Dan said. "Not personal."

"You didn't come all the way out here to look for me, did you?" Hutton wanted to know. "I'll bet Lucy Green sent you, didn't she?"

Dan smiled. "What makes you think Lucy Green cares where you are?"

Hutton glared at Dan. "Because she just called for me. But I don't answer to her, so I told the barmaid to tell her I wasn't here."

"What does that matter?" Dan said. "I told you this was official business. I've got some questions I want to ask you."

"Well, it's a good thing you picked here to ask them," Hutton went on. His chin stuck out at Dan while he talked. "As of tonight, I'm running the Green Ranch. If you don't believe me, ask Martha Green."

"What does Lucy have to say about that?" Dan asked.

Hutton stiffened. "Lucy doesn't have anything to say about it, Slayter. It was Martha who offered me the position. So you're no longer welcome out there."

Dan ignored the comment. "I came in here looking for Brice Foster. I don't suppose any of you have seen him this evening."

"I don't suppose," Hutton said. "I heard on the news he shot a man. One of the Cross Twelve hands is what somebody said. I thought he was working for them."

"I just want to know if you've seen him, that's all," Dan said.

"And I told you I haven't," Hutton retorted. "He knows better than to show up at the Green Ranch ever again. His days on Canyon Mountain are over."

"You just tend to watching the ranch, if that's really what you're doing," Dan told Hutton. "Barlow and the rest of them are my responsibility."

"Then you just keep your responsibility there, and not with Lucy Green," Hutton said. "There are a lot more people besides Big Jed Barlow and the Cross Twelve hands who would like to see you out of the way."

Dan again ignored Hutton. He realized he wasn't going to get anywhere with him. What bothered him most was Hutton's claim to be running the Green Ranch for Martha. That couldn't be true. Dan didn't think much of the remark because Hutton was always spouting off about being the big shot of something—and it was never true.

But this time Hutton seemed to have an air of authority about him that puzzled Dan and made him wonder. Surely Lucy wouldn't stand for that.

Dan asked a couple of the barmaids and a few more of the people in attendance if they had seen a man who fit Foster's description. No one had and Dan decided to leave.

Before going back to his Jeep, Dan decided to call the Cross 12 and tell Big Jed Barlow that one of his ranch pickups had been abandoned along the road near Chico. Dan had no intention of letting Barlow come and take it, as there was a lot of evidence in that pickup that needed to be gathered before it was even moved.

Dan's intention was to feel Barlow out and to see what his mood was like. Barlow had certainly heard about the incident on the highway by now, and the death of Jim Weller, so there would be no surprise there. What Dan hoped to accomplish was to get an idea if Barlow wanted to give up his quest for the Green Ranch, or go full speed ahead.

Dan let the phone ring for a dozen times. He hung up and hurried to his Jeep. Barlow should be home this time of night, but he was gone. Everyone was gone. There should have been somebody there.

When Dan got into his Jeep, the dispatcher was calling him over his radio. Dan answered and the dispatcher seemed to be in a frenzy.

"I've been trying to get hold of you for some time," she said. "Urgent message awaits your arrival back at the office."

Dan knew without asking. "10-4," he said. "Would the message have to do with Lucy Green?"

The dispatcher answered in the affirmative. Dan then told her to have Leon come on the radio. He told Leon to take as many deputies as he could and meet him at the Green Ranch. Leon told Dan he was on his way.

Dan sped off in the Jeep, knowing the answer to his question about whether or not Barlow intended to go after the Green Ranch now. Dan thought to himself that he should have known that Barlow's intentions would never change — and that this might be the night he would try and make his plan work.

Chapter Sixteen

Lucy and Martha saddled the horses by starlight. They both realized they had little time to reach the top of the mountain before Big Jed Barlow and his men beat them up from the other side. But theirs was a much shorter ride and they just hoped they could get there in time to save the bull.

Martha had been pleading with Lucy to leave the rifle behind. But Lucy would not listen. She knew there was no way they could hope to outgun Barlow and his men. Instead, she thought that they might pull a trick on them that would discourage rustling—at least for one more night.

Just before leaving, Lucy found two hatchets in the barn. There was plenty of wood up on the mountain and it was Lucy's reasoning that if it took a fire to keep the wolves away, then she would build a big one.

Lucy and Martha rode hard through the darkness, slowing down only at the narrow crossing that snaked past the edge of the cliff. Then once on top, they set to work as fast as they could. They gathered wood from downed timber and chopped it into pieces. Then they set to building a fire near the corrals.

The blaze quickly rose into the night sky. It scared some of the cattle that had bedded down nearby and they moved off into the night. But there were some of the herd that remained and Lucy could see the big Charolais bull was among those who did not wander too far away.

"We've got to keep our eye on that bull," Lucy said. "We can't let the Barlows near him."

"Let's just hope the Barlows and their hands leave," Martha said.

It was their hope that the fire would deter the Barlows and make them think something was going on that could mess up their rustling plans. Lucy knew she could not afford to let the Barlows and the Cross 12 hands know that just the two of them were up here trying to stand them all off with a silly campfire.

Once the fire was going, Lucy and Martha hid themselves and their horses off on the south side of the meadow. From their position they could see the bull easily and also watch for riders coming up the trail from the Cross 12 side of the mountain.

What would make their plan work was to have nobody near the fire and hopefully make the Barlows wonder what was going on; who had built the fire, why, and whether there were a lot of men waiting for them or not.

It wasn't long until Lucy and Martha saw Big Jed Barlow leading his brother and the Cross 12 hands up from the trail on the north side and into the meadow. From the shadows, they could see Big Jed hold everyone up and stare out across the meadow at the flickering fire.

"What if they see us?" Martha asked.

"They won't see us, Mother," Lucy said. "I want you to take it easy. I knew I shouldn't have let you come up here with me."

"I'll be fine," Martha said. "I just hope they leave."

"I think they will," Lucy said. She was pointing across to Big Jed, who appeared to be putting something to his mouth. "I think he's got a radio. Maybe he's telling the helicopter not to come in."

Out in the night sky, the helicopter was just a strange form in the black that moved and then seemed to come to a halt in midair before turning and going out of sight. Soon the sky was only stars again and Martha and Lucy tried to hold back their enthusiasm.

"We did it!" Lucy said. "The trick worked."

While they watched awhile longer, Lucy and Martha could see Big Jed Barlow talking with his brother, Chet, and some of his hands before he turned them all around and rode back down the mountain.

Lucy could barely contain her joy. She hugged her mother and jumped up and down in the darkness.

"Yes, I think they've left," Martha said. "Let's put that fire out and go on down the mountain."

Lucy detected something in her mother's voice,

something that sounded like pain.

"How are you feeling, Mother?" she asked.

"I'm fine," Martha answered. "Let's get that fire put out."

Lucy could tell that her mother was starting to suffer in the chest area again. Martha was starting to slump some. It was her heart. Now Lucy began to worry and she asked her mother again if she was getting sick at all.

"I told you, I'm fine," Martha said. She swung up onto her horse and began to ride across the meadow toward the corrals.

Lucy followed on her palomino and got down near the water trough.

"Mother, let me put the fire out," Lucy said. "I don't want you lifting anything."

"With two of us it will go that much faster," Martha said. "The sooner the fire is put out, the sooner we get down this mountain."

Lucy worked with her mother to haul pails of water to the fire. It sizzled and spat as the flames and coals were doused over and over again until each tiny spark was eliminated.

"That should do it," Lucy finally said.

"Time to go home," her mother agreed.

Lucy took the reins to her horse and her eye caught what she perceived to be movement a way off at the edge of the timber. A deer, she thought. But it seemed too big for a deer. She turned to her mother, but decided not to say anything—not until she was absolutely sure of what she saw.

Lucy took one more look at the edge of the trees

and thought she saw a horse go into the timber and disappear. It appeared to have a rider on its back. How could that be? She asked herself the question over and over. She wondered if she had really seen a horse and rider or if it had been her imagination.

When Lucy turned back to her mother once again, she found her leaning against the corral poles with her hand over her chest. Her attention went from the rider out in the darkness to her mother.

"Mother! Are you all right?" she asked.

"My chest hurts," Martha Green said. "Oh, God, how it hurts."

Lucy fought alarm. She helped her mother to turn from the corral and get hold of her horse. Lucy then pushed her up into the saddle and climbed on Lady. She realized that her mother's heart was once again craving oxygen, that the excitement had made her breathe too fast and had caused her metabolism to rise too fast once again.

And the added strain of carrying water to put out the fire hadn't done a bit of good. She should have forced her mother to just stand back and let well enough alone. Now Lucy worried about getting her mother down the mountain and to the hospital before she died.

"Mother, I want you to take deep breaths," Lucy said. "Please try to relax and just take deep breaths."

"I'm so tired," Lucy's mother said. "I feel like I could go to sleep."

"Please hold on," Lucy said. "Just hold on to the horse and don't go to sleep. I don't want you to fall off."

Lucy led her mother's horse down off Canyon Mountain in the darkness. They went over the narrow trail along the cliff and Lucy held her breath as her mother's horse slipped once, but regained its balance before it slid down to the edge. The night sky was filling with clouds and the trail was becoming more obscure. Lucy tried to hurry the horses—she knew there wasn't much time.

"How are you doing, Mother?" she called back.

"I'm here," her mother answered. "But we had better hurry. I can hear horses not far behind us."

Lucy then listened and concluded that Big Jed Barlow and his men had discovered them and were coming down the mountain not far behind. The rider she thought she had seen in the shadows had indeed been real. Now she and her mother had to move fast. If Barlow and his men caught up to them, Lucy knew their lives would be in danger. Big Jed Barlow could not afford to have any witnesses to crimes he had committed.

After riding but a short way farther, Lucy realized they were never going to be able to outrun Big Jed Barlow and his men. It would be hopeless to think they could get away, especially with her mother's heart problem acting up. She was barely able to stay on her horse, much less ride hard.

"Mother, you keep going down toward the ranch," Lucy said. "I'm going to have to keep

Barlow and his men from catching us."

"Lucy, what are you going to do?" Martha asked.

"You just ride on down the mountain and don't worry about me," Lucy said.

"I'm not going without you," Martha said. "I couldn't go back wondering what had happened to you."

"I have to keep them from getting to us," Lucy said. "That means using the rifle. I don't want you getting in the line of fire."

"I told you, I'm not going back without you," Martha said.

Lucy helped her mother into cover nearby and told her to remain there until she got back. Then Lucy worked her way back up the trail a short way to where the high cliff worked its way around the mountain. She could hear Big Jed Barlow and his men coming down the trail toward the cliff and she knew this was the place to stop them.

"Don't try to come across the trail along the cliff!" Lucy yelled out to them in the darkness. "I won't let you come. Go on back, the sheriff is on his way."

Lucy wondered if Barlow would believe her lie about Dan Slayter coming. As far as she knew, Dan was still chasing Brice Foster and hadn't gotten the message concerning what was happening up on the mountain. She could only hope Barlow would decide to turn back and leave the mountain.

Instead, there came a hail of gunfire from somewhere in the darkness on the other side of the trail.

Lucy ducked as bullets zipped through the trees around her. She could see the long licks of flame that came from the Cross 12 rifles. She became angry then and pulled back the hammer on her own rifle.

She fired in the general direction of the flame that spat from just across the cliff. She fired a number of times and noticed that the shooting from Big Jed Barlow and the Cross 12 hands had stopped. She reloaded her rifle and waited for more firing to start up.

When she thought she saw movement in the shadows at the edge of the trail, she fired once again. She thought she heard someone yell and she fired again in the direction of the sound.

Lucy made sure her rifle was loaded again and waited. Now there was no sound from the trees. She moved slowly along the trail, taking her time as she went out onto the ledge of the cliff. She stayed low to the ground to avoid being seen and her heart thumped in her chest. She wasn't going to let Big Jed Barlow do just whatever he wanted.

When she got across the cliff, Lucy looked out over the open meadow at the top of the mountain. At the far end, where the moon made a faint glow of light near the trail that went down, Lucy could see Big Jed Barlow and the Cross 12 hands going out. She had succeeded in driving them off the mountain.

Lucy hurried back to find her mother breathing more normally. She was frightened, but she seemed to be doing better.

"Lucy, I thought they'd killed you," she said.

"Is that why you're breathing easier?" Lucy said with a laugh.

Martha had to laugh then as well. "No, I was just sitting here thinking that I couldn't do anything one way or the other, so I'd just as well try and relax. I couldn't see any reason in killing myself if I could help it."

"Big Jed Barlow and the Cross Twelve hands are gone, at least for tonight," Lucy said. "I'm sure they won't give up, though."

"Probably not," Martha agreed. She let Lucy help her back on her horse. "But at least you won't be doing it alone next time."

"I hope not," Lucy said.

They started back down the mountain and Lucy felt better about her mother. She seemed to have come to some conclusion.

"I've come to realize something," Martha said. "I believe you're right; we don't need Ben Hutton to help run this ranch. We don't need him at all—not while there's the two of us."

Lucy laughed. "Now you're talking, Mother. We can run the ranch together, just the two of us. I don't understand why you felt we needed Ben Hutton."

"Ben told me he loved you," Martha said. "He said he loved you very much. I just thought if he cared that much for you, he could help us."

"He doesn't care that much for me, believe me, Mother," Lucy said. "I think he's just out to get something for nothing, namely our ranch."

"Maybe you're right," Martha said. "But you have to understand, I've lived a lot of years with a man around the house. It's hard to get used to not having one, especially when he's taken away from you the way your father was taken from me."

"I can understand, Mother," Lucy said. "But you are old enough now not to have to worry about anybody providing for you. We have a lot of land and when we get the Cross Twelve off our backs, we can expand."

"Do you think we'll ever get the Cross Twelve off our backs?" Martha asked.

"Yes," Lucy answered. "One way or another we will. And then we're really going to live it up."

Chapter Seventeen

Dan met Leon and a team of deputies at the Green Ranch just as Lucy was bringing her mother down to the corrals. The sun was just starting to rise, and the sky in the east was saturated with gold. Dan was relieved to see them and told them he had come as fast as he could.

"Did you get Brice Foster?" Lucy asked.

"No," Dan answered. "Foster managed to leave the pickup he took along the road to Chico and lose himself up in the timber. I was hoping to get a search team together. But I don't know which is more important, doing that or watching Canyon Mountain."

"I know Barlow will be back soon," Lucy said. "We're lucky we're here right now."

"What do you mean?" Dan asked.

Lucy told Dan what had happened up on the mountain and how she had managed to keep Big Jed Barlow and the Cross 12 hands from catching up with them.

"You can't fight Big Jed Barlow yourself," Dan said.

"We didn't have a choice," Lucy pointed out. "It was either that or lose our ranch. Do you understand?"

"There's a lot I need to understand," Dan said. "Let's start with my getting some information from you. Who and what did you see up there?"

"It was dark," Lucy said. "It was hard to see anything. We built a fire and when we saw Big Jed Barlow—I know it was Big Jed—riding along the opposite edge of the meadow, we prayed he would call off the rustling attempt. He and his hands talked for a while and we saw the helicopter turn around in midair and move off. Then Barlow and his men came after us."

"Did you get a good look at Barlow at any time during this whole thing?" Dan asked.

"I didn't have to see his face to know it was him," Lucy said. "There aren't many men his size in this entire state."

"Your mother must have been in bad shape by then," Dan said. "What kept Barlow and his men from catching you?"

"I can shoot a rifle," Lucy said flatly.

"Did you hit any of them?"

"I hope to God I did. I heard one of them yell. But I can't be sure if he was hit."

"What about the bull and the rest of the herd?"

Lucy shrugged. "They were still there when I left with Mother. But who knows what has happened since then."

Dan turned his hat around in his hands, thinking. He moved to the window and looked out into the mountain country at the edge of town.

"I've got to get a search team organized to look for Brice Foster," he said. "I think it would be a good idea if you took your mother into the hospital for the day, if nothing else then just for observation—just to be safe."

"What about the ranch?" Lucy asked.

"Where's Ben Hutton?" Dan said. "He told me at Chico last night that he was the ramrod here now."

"I need to have a talk with him," Lucy said. "Mother told him something and now she's changed her mind."

"Let's get her into town," Dan said. "You can worry about Hutton later."

Dan took both Martha and Lucy in his Jeep and though Martha wasn't anxious to spend the day in the hospital, she agreed to. Her chest was sore and she didn't want to suffer any more problems with her heart.

Dan left Lucy with her mother at the hospital and began organizing the search effort for Foster. Dan and Leon and a team of five deputies arrived at Chico soon after ten in the morning and Dan organized a ride by the deputies through the mountains behind the resort.

While they rode, Dan took off from the place where the pickup had been left at the side of the road. Tracking Foster was easy for a time; there was plenty of broken grass and boot marks in the soil. But higher up in the timber, Dan lost the trail.

Foster had been smart to stick to the rocky

country, where he could walk from rock to rock without leaving tracks. Dan found himself high up with no trace of where Foster might be or what he was up to. The one thing Dan did know was that sooner or later he would try to link up with Big Jed Barlow again. And they would then try to once and for all put the Green Ranch out of business.

Though the hand Lucy Green had shot was not seriously injured, Big Jed Barlow was furious that the plan to take the bull off the mountain hadn't worked. Somehow Lucy Green had gotten the courage to start shooting at the most strategic place along the trail down the mountain. There had been no choice but to turn back—especially if Slayter had been on his way up.

But now Barlow was beginning to wonder if Slayter had been on his way or not. It didn't really matter, for the night had passed already and daylight was coming. They couldn't take a bull out by helicopter in the light.

And speaking of truth and lies, what about Brice Foster? He had just called in to tell Big Jed that he was hiding just above Chico Hot Springs, and that there were a whole lot of lawmen looking for him. He didn't know where the cabin was, but he was hiding out near a campground.

"We can't come up there to get you now," Big Jed had told him. "That would be too obvious. You're going to have to make it hiding out a couple of days. And I want to know what happened with Weller."

Foster had told Big Jed that he had killed Jim Weller out of necessity.

"It was him or me," Foster had told Barlow. "Slayter was coming up the road and Weller put a gun on me and told me to get out, that he didn't want anything to do with Slayter. So I tried to take the gun away from him and it went off. It was an accident."

"How could he hold a gun on you when he was driving?" Barlow had asked.

Foster had begun to talk fast then. "No, I was driving. Weller got tired and I drove. He was holding the gun on me and I reached over. It went off."

"We'll send somebody up to get you day after tomorrow," Foster had then said. "Be at Chico late in the afternoon."

At this point Barlow didn't care whether or not Foster was telling the truth. He just wanted that last bull down off the mountain. He had to get that bull down now; he had too much invested in trying to get the Green Ranch to throw it all away now.

He was paying the pilot a fortune to keep his helicopter in hiding in the back country between Red Lodge and Cooke City. Day after tomorrow he was flying in again, no questions asked. It would be dark and there would be a bull to pick up. Either that or the pilot was on his way back to Canada, and he wouldn't be back.

* * *

It was late afternoon and Dan was standing at the window that overlooked the mountains in Martha Green's hospital room. Her heart was weaker than they had first thought and she would be in the hospital at least for another two or three days.

Martha Green was now asleep and in no real danger. Dan had been talking to Lucy about the day and how they hadn't been able to locate Brice Foster.

"He's up there," Dan said. "But he's good at hiding out. I think he's had a lot of experience."

"How are you going to find him?" Lucy asked.

"I think he's bound to come to Big Jed Barlow sooner or later," Dan said. "Barlow hired him to change brands on cattle. That's why he's here. It seems to me that Barlow wants him around to get the job done on Canyon Mountain."

"It all comes down to that, doesn't it?" Lucy said. "Canyon Mountain will make or break either Mother and me, or Big Red Barlow and the Cross Twelve Ranch."

"It looks that way," Dan said. "I'm going to take a ride up there and see what I can find out. Maybe Barlow and his men left some more evidence — just enough to piece this together and get them put behind bars."

Lucy followed him out of the hospital room and stopped him in the hall.

"I'm going up there with you," she said.

"Your mother needs you here," Dan said.

"She's doing all right," Lucy argued. "She's stable and you're wrong, there's nothing I can do for her now. Besides, I want to show you where I saw Barlow and his men come up the mountain and where they were riding when Mother and I watched them."

"What about the hands you hired?" Dan said. "What about Hutton?"

"He stopped by here today and I told him to go back to the ranch and to pack his things," Lucy said. "He told me he didn't take orders from me, that he took them from Mother. Of course, I had to get a doctor to persuade him not to wake her up. But he left mad, anyway. And he said that he was sick and tired of me playing up to you."

"It sounds to me like he wants to stop Big Jed Barlow by himself and hopefully get in your good graces then," Dan said.

"I don't care if he did succeed in stopping Barlow by himself," Lucy said. "That wouldn't change my mind about him."

Dan called into the office and notified the dispatcher that he was going out to the Green Ranch, and to relay the message to Leon. Leon and some of the deputies were still above Chico on the search for Foster, but Dan wanted him to be ready to come to Canyon Mountain with backup help if needed.

He got into his Jeep and followed Lucy out to the ranch. When they got there, Dan noticed that Lucy was angry about something.

She got out of her car and stood with her hands on her hips, looking out toward the corrals. Dan got out and walked over to her.

"What's bothering you?" he asked.

"It looks like Hutton didn't take anything I said to heart this morning," she said. "I see he's gone off somewhere on that speckled roan he's sort of taken over as his own. I wonder where he is, and what he thinks he's doing."

"Probably a one man army headed for the Cross Twelve," Dan said. "I wonder where the rest of your hands are."

"They stayed in Chico," Lucy said. "Hutton told me that this morning. I don't know if they think working for the Green Ranch is one big party or what."

"We can still ride up on Canyon Mountain," Dan said. "I'll see what evidence I can gather. It's getting pretty late in the day, but I think I'll have enough time to get some valuable information."

Dan made sure his pistol was loaded and his rifle had a bullet ready to lever into the barrel. Then he followed Lucy to the corrals and picked out a big sorrel stallion. She had her little palomino mare and together they set out on the trail that wound up Canyon Mountain.

They reached the top of the mountain with less than an hour of daylight left. The Green Ranch cattle were watering at the stock tank closest to the corrals, chewing their cuds lazily and wandering around. They had been grazing most of the day and were ready to bed down for the night.

The Charolais bull was with them and Lucy was relieved to see that the animal was in good shape.

He was a prize bull and well worth fifty thousand dollars. A man as greedy as Barlow would be after a bull like that until he got him.

Dan worked fast, moving back and forth across the meadow, looking closely at the signs he saw everywhere. There were horse tracks that did not match either Martha's or Lucy's horse, and there were cigarette butts lying here and there. Dan found an empty package and put it in a bag for fingerprinting.

"I don't know how you intend to catch them unless you're up here when they try to steal cattle," Lucy said. "Fingerprints and tracks and all that stuff doesn't seem to really help you. I don't know why you bother."

"It might prove valuable later, after I take Big Jed Barlow in and need additional evidence to prove he has been in this pasture," Dan explained. "You don't know how hard it is to get a strong conviction in court."

"Oh, yes, I do," Lucy said. "We've been fighting the Barlows for a hundred years and I can't remember any stories told by my dad or grandfather that talk about any of those outlaws going to jail. They're way too sneaky. And they hire lawyers that show them the legal loopholes."

"Sooner or later people like that make mistakes," Dan said. "It happens every time; someone gets too cocky and suddenly they expose themselves. That will happen to Big Jed Barlow sooner or later."

"Have you got what you came for?" Lucy asked.

"I think I've got as much as I can get for now," Dan said. The shadows next to the ground had made searching nearly impossible. "Let me just look around the corrals once more."

Dan spent a short time looking around for additional evidence. He found a few empty cartridge casings, but nothing more. There was little left for him to do now.

There came a slight breeze up on the mountain and the heat from the day began to move. It was quickly replaced by cooler air that slipped down from the high Gallatins to the west. Dan leaned against the corral, looking out into the western sky. There was just a streak of red left as the night came into the valley.

Lucy watched Dan standing with his hands folded in front of him and walked over. She put a hand on his shoulder and looked up into his eyes.

"You're different, aren't you?" she said. "You like sunsets and range flowers, and yet you were a champion college wrestler. What is it that makes you tick?"

"I'm just me," Dan said with a shrug. "There's a lot of people who don't like that. But they think I can be their sheriff. That's how people are: they don't always like you for who you are but as long as you're doing something they approve of, they leave you alone."

Lucy leaned forward to put her arms around his neck. She slipped and started to go down, but Dan leaned over and caught her. Just as he leaned over a rifle sounded and a bullet slammed into a corral post right where his chest had been.

Dan pushed Lucy under the lowest corral pole and into the corral as more shots came and zipped into the grass around them. When he saw that Lucy was safe, Dan grabbed his rifle in the grass and moved around the edge of the corral.

He levered a bullet into the chamber and peered into the blackness to look for flashes of light from a rifle barrel. But the shooting had stopped. He heard instead the sound of a horse running nearby and looked out into the meadow to see a black shape moving through the shadows. In the last bit of twilight, he could see a rider leaning over the horse's back.

Dan leveled the rifle and aimed just ahead of the running horse and just above its head. But it was too dark and he decided not to chance a shot.

After lowering the hammer against the chamber, Dan waited for more riders to appear. But there was only the whisper of the wind and the jerky, scared breathing of Lucy as she remained down in the grass.

"I can't figure who that would have been," Dan finally said. "But I think we had better get down off the mountain, just in case that rider was one of Barlow's hands. He might go back for help."

Lucy got up and dusted herself off. The shock was still with her and it was a moment before she could talk.

"I don't understand that," she said. "Why would Ben Hutton want to kill you?"

"Ben Hutton?" Dan said.

Lucy nodded. "Remember when we first got to the ranch? I told you the horse that Ben Hutton used to ride was missing. I couldn't figure where he was. Hutton was up here, waiting for us."

"Hutton is supposed to be on our side," Dan said.

"Ben Hutton is for himself, no one else," Lucy said. "He wants me and he wants the ranch. He thinks if he gets rid of you and makes it look like Barlow did it, he would be justified in going after Barlow. If you want to know, I think Ben Hutton has gone off the deep end."

Dan nodded. He and Lucy got on their horses and started back down off the mountain. It was completely dark, but the sky was clear and a half-moon was rising over the valley. Dan told Lucy that she should seek a restraining order to keep Hutton off the ranch.

"He won't pay any attention to that," Lucy said.

"He will if it means going to jail," Dan said.

Dan rode on down with Lucy, watching the shadows carefully and making sure they didn't ride anywhere they could be caught in an ambush. As they rode, Dan thought about Hutton and realized that Lucy was right—Hutton had gotten himself in very deep and he was so desperate to make himself a hero. Dan knew it was up to him to stop Hutton as soon as he could, before he did something that would do a lot of people a lot of harm.

Chapter Eighteen

Ben Hutton spent the following day lounging around Chico with the Green Ranch hands. He had come down off Canyon Mountain the night before, wishing he had connected on his shot at Dan Slayter. But maybe he would get another chance.

He hadn't worried about coming down off the mountain, as he knew Lucy was in town staying at the hospital with her mother. And he knew Slayter was busy keeping the search for Brice Foster organized.

It was now late afternoon and Hutton and the Green Ranch cowhands were lined against the bar in the Chico Saloon. There were a few tourists sitting around at the tables and one at the bar, reading a copy of the Billings *Gazette*. A good number were swimming in the hot springs pool, as the evening was cooling down with a flow of air down off the high country.

The bar had its typical atmosphere for a midsummer's evening: laid-back and casual, with the usual comings and goings of locals and tourists together. The juke box was going and Merle Haggard was singing a song about being somewhere in the middle of Montana — somewhere free from the complexities of everyday life. Ben Hutton knew as he listened to the song that when the Cross 12 boys came in, life was going to get very interesting.

Hutton and the Green Ranch hands drank a couple rounds before a number of the Cross 12 cowhands came in the door. They looked around as if they were supposed to meet somebody there, and finally settled down at a table and ordered beers.

Hutton could see that the Green Ranch hands he was with were acquainted with a couple of the Cross 12 hands. They didn't appear to like one another very well and it showed.

In a matter of but a few minutes Brice Foster came in the door. Foster stopped as he came in and stared. It was as if he had hit a brick wall. He had no idea he was going to run into Ben Hutton and the hands from the Green Ranch.

Ben Hutton and the Green Ranch hands watched the Cross 12 cowhands talking to Foster. Foster's surprise had by now turned to aggression and he immediately went to the pool table and put some money in.

The Cross 12 hands got up and tried to talk Foster out of playing pool. They were whispering, but loud enough so that Hutton could hear them telling Foster he had more important things to do.

Hutton knew what Foster was up to but he remained at the bar, sipping at his drink. As the

191

balls fell into the tray and Foster racked them, all the hands from both the Cross 12 and the Green Ranch began to grow tense.

"Thought I'd see if I couldn't get my money back from you," Foster finally said to Ben Hutton. "That is, unless you think you can't take me twice in a row."

Hutton set his drink down on the bar and went to the rack of pool cues along the wall.

"There isn't a day in heaven or hell that I can't beat your ass flat down," he said.

Foster stopped chalking his cue and glared at Hutton. The muscles in his face were set tight. Everyone in the room watched him. Finally he went back to chalking his cue.

"Why don't we make it twenty bucks a game, Hutton?" he said. "Or maybe you can't afford it."

"Make it easy on yourself," Hutton said. He put a twenty dollar bill out next to Foster's.

Foster rolled the cue ball up to the front of the table from where it was resting near the racked balls.

"Lag for first shot."

Foster watched while Hutton shot the cue ball down to the end of the table against the far cushion and then kept his eye on the white ball until it came to a stop back up at the other end just a few inches from the front cushion.

"See if you can beat that lag," Hutton said with a laugh.

Foster moved over and lowered his stick and tapped the cue ball toward the other end. The ball came off the far cushion and came to rest nearly against the front cushion. Foster then turned to Hutton and grinned.

"Looks like I break," he said. "You bring your checkbook?"

Ben Hutton showed no expression. He watched while Foster broke the balls and ran the table down to three remaining, including the eight ball. Then Hutton sank two of the balls and missed the shot at the eight, leaving Foster set up with an easy shot to win the game.

"That's really too bad," Foster said. "I gave you a chance and you blew it."

Hutton dug in his pocket and found another twenty. Except for the juke box, the barroom remained quiet. Hutton racked the balls and watched Foster run the table and then put the eight ball down as well. Foster grinned. He then took Hutton's money and put it in his pocket.

"What the hell are you doing?" Hutton asked. "I haven't had a chance to shoot yet."

"What do you mean?" Foster said. "You don't get a chance to shoot. I won the game."

"You get to rack the balls," Hutton said, "and if I don't run the table, you win."

"No, I already won," Foster argued.

"The hell you did!" Hutton yelled. He suddenly moved around the table and swung his pool cue at Foster.

As the cue came toward him from over the top, Foster dodged sideways and the cue hit and cracked on the edge of the table. But Hutton brought the cue up again right away and swung again, glancing a blow off Foster's raised forearm. Foster grabbed Hutton's arm before he could swing again and wrestled him to the floor.

The hands from both ranches were now up and at one another, using fists and beer bottles and chairs. They smashed through tables and broke the poker machines along the wall. A few of the men even ended up going through the glass door and onto the concrete at the edge of the outdoor pool, scaring the swimmers into leaving.

When the security guards showed up, all they could do was watch and be sure that the sheriff's office had been notified. There were way too many men for them to handle.

Hutton and Foster were still fighting near the pool table. Brice Foster had managed to open a deep cut over Ben Hutton's right eye and Hutton was blinded in that eye by a heavy stream of blood that trailed out of the eyebrow and down across his face. He was cursing and trying to ward off more blows from Foster. He finally managed to lunge into Foster and knock him off balance.

Hutton then pinned Foster against the pool table and began pummelling him with his fists. Foster fell back over the pool table and Hutton grabbed him by the hair and slammed his head into the table repeatedly, staining the felt top with blood and hair.

From somewhere outside came the sounds of gunfire. Hutton stopped beating on Foster and went to a broken window to see who was shooting.

Outside, it was getting close to dark and small crowds of tourists who had been drawn toward the bar by the brawl were running and screaming.

Hutton could see long licks of flame coming from gun barrels behind pickups. Bullets whined off metal and smashed through window and windshield glass. The hands from both ranches had taken their fight into the parking lot, and resumed it with rifles.

Hutton turned back to the pool table. Foster was on his hands and knees, shaking his head. Hutton turned and ran from the saloon into the parking lot, where he grabbed a rifle from his pickup.

Two Cross 12 hands went down as he began firing and he yelled with glee. He was going to rid the country of Big Jed Barlow and his cowhands all by himself.

Foster got up and cleared his head. The fighting outside was intense and he knew he had to get out of there before the law arrived—either that or go to jail for an awful long time.

Without hesitation, Foster then ran from the bar and made his way along the edge of the building toward one of the Cross 12 pickups. He was nearly hit by rifle fire twice, but managed to get to the truck and leave. He knew his best choice was to go straight to the Cross 12 Ranch and face Big Jed Barlow. It was time to get out of Montana.

Dan turned his Jeep up the secondary highway

that led to Chico. His lights were flashing and his siren blaring. Close behind him were two other vehicles filled with deputies. All of them were heavily armed.

Leon was in Dan's Jeep on the passenger side, shaking his head.

"Man, I knew it would come to this," he was saying. "Them two ranches just want to wipe each other out completely."

The call had come from a badly distressed bartender who had taken a piece of flying wood against her head. She had called from a pay phone next to the bathrooms and the noise from the fight had been so great in the background that the dispatcher could hardly make out what she was saying.

Luckily, Dan and Leon and the other deputies had just given up their search for Foster and were only a short way down the road from Chico when the call had come over the radio. As it was, they pulled into the parking lot at Chico Hot Springs to find a major gun battle going on.

The shooting slowed somewhat at the sound of the sirens. But Dan could see both sides were determined to get rid of one another. Dan's yelling for them to cease firing and put their hands above their heads did nothing to stop most of them, including Ben Hutton.

Hutton was now in the trees, firing with his rifle at two Cross 12 hands under cover behind a pickup. Hutton was a wild man, racing out from the trees to shoot and back in again to reload.

196

Again Dan yelled for the shooting to stop and spread his deputies out to get ready to fire themselves. At this, the hired hands from both ranches dropped their guns and yelled that they were surrendering.

Hutton finally stopped shooting from the trees. Dan could see that he was turning upslope in an effort to get away. Dan told Leon to take charge of the arrests and gave chase, realizing that if Hutton got away now he might never get another chance like this at him.

Though Hutton had a good head start, he stood no chance of getting away from Dan. Hutton climbed hard up the slope to get to the top but Dan climbed harder and faster, his energy much higher than Hutton's.

Near the top, Hutton turned to shoot at Dan. But he was too tired to get a bullet levered into the barrel before Dan reached him.

Hutton cursed and swung the butt end of the rifle at Dan, who ducked and pulled the rifle away from him. As Hutton turned to try and run again, Dan caught him by the back of the shirt and spun him around.

Dan's fist slammed hard into Hutton's mouth, knocking his head back. Hutton fell down hard into the grass and pine needles along the slope. Dan told him to stay put but Hutton screamed more curses and got up swinging.

Without mercy, Dan brought a fist heavily into Hutton's midsection, doubling him over. Dan then pulled Hutton's head back by the hair and smashed a right cross into his jaw. The bone cracked and Hutton went down, unconscious.

Dan picked up Hutton's rifle and then took him by the collar of his shirt and began to drag him downhill. Near the bottom, Hutton regained consciousness and struggled to get free of Dan's grasp. Dan allowed Hutton to get to his feet.

"Your best bet is to settle down," Dan said. "Or maybe you'd rather try to run again."

Hutton glared, holding his jaw. He wanted to curse again but the pain in his face was too great. He knew his jaw was broken and that he was going to jail just as soon as he left the doctor's office.

Hutton watched while Dan talked to Leon and the other deputies, who had already called in for medical help and backup. There were men from both ranches lying in the parking lot and at least five of them had coats over their faces. In the fading light of day, Ben Hutton realized he had blown all the chances he had for making things up to Lucy Green.

Hutton sat against the wheel well of the Jeep and let his head clear more. He knew that Dan Slayter, just a few steps away, was getting ready to turn around and have him stand up so he could put handcuffs on him. The ambulances with the injured hands from both ranches were on their way in to the hospital. Hutton knew he had to act now, before the other ambulance arrived to take him to the hospital.

Dan was just noticing the extra ambulance coming into the parking lot when Hutton jumped up from where he had been sitting against the Jeep. Dan saw Hutton moving quickly toward the edge of the parking lot and then saw him stop and pick something up from the grass along the slope.

Even before Hutton could turn with the rifle, Dan had his pistol drawn and was yelling a warning to Hutton. But Hutton wasn't listening. Hutton turned to fire the rifle and Dan's revolver spit a long streak of red. Hutton dropped the rifle and pitched forward into the gravel of the parking lot.

Leon and the other deputies kept the crowd back and the prisoners under control as Dan walked over to Hutton. One of Hutton's legs was twitching and the fingers on his right hand were moving slowly, but soon he lay still while a pool of blood formed beneath him and soaked into the roadway.

Dan talked to Leon for a while and learned that Brice Foster had been in on the whole thing, and had in fact started it all. The Cross 12 hands had come to Chico to pick him up and he had insisted on playing pool against Hutton.

"Did any of them say where Foster is now?" Dan asked Leon.

Leon nodded. "They said he took off in a pickup."

"Well, I guess we know where he's headed, don't we?" Dan said. "We'd better get to Canyon Mountain before Foster makes it to the Cross Twelve. Otherwise, we'll be too late to save the Green Ranch."

Chapter Nineteen

Big Jed Barlow paced the floor of the ranch house and cursed. Brice Foster and the rest of the hands hadn't returned from Chico and it was nearly midnight. They should have returned long before now. Now he was in a bind and to make it worse, he had to listen to Chet tell him that Foster was a big curse of bad luck—that he should have gotten rid of Foster when he had the chance.

Big Jed yelled at Chet to quiet down and picked up the phone again. He had tried calling the saloon frequently but kept getting a busy signal. Finally he decided to try the lodge.

On the second ring a young woman answered and when Barlow asked her if there was some way she could connect him with the bar, she said the bar was closed down for repairs.

"Repairs?" Barlow said.

"Yes," the young woman replied. "There was a terrible fight in there tonight. And shooting outside. The saloon is closed for repairs and the sheriff's office is out here still."

Barlow paused, unable to believe what he was hearing. Finally he asked, "Can you tell me who was involved?"

"I'm afraid not," the young woman said, "I'm not allowed to discuss any of what went on. I'm sorry."

Barlow slammed the phone down and cursed again. He was sure now that Foster had somehow gotten himself into something. Foster had never been late for a job before, especially when it involved expensive cattle to be rustled. Something had definitely happened. And if it involved the sheriff's office, it had to be major.

Chet seemed to sense the news was the worst.

"What the hell happened?" he asked. "Did Foster run into the Green Ranch hands or something?"

"Or something is right," Big Jed said. "I guess they had a hell of a fight. The sheriff's department is still out there."

"What about Foster?" Chet asked.

Big Jed shrugged. "I don't know. And I don't know where the rest of our hands are, either."

"We can't wait for them," Chet said. "If the sheriff is out at Chico and so are the Green Ranch hands, we should move now. Let's get the rest of the hands and get up on that mountain right away. We can get that bull, with or without Foster. Dan Slayter will be all night at Chico sorting things

201

out."

"That should make it easier," Big Jed said. "The helicopter is supposed to be up there in about three hours."

"We're going to get this done without Foster," Chet told Big Jed again. "That's the way it should have been from the beginning. You know that, don't you?"

Big Jed was standing at the gun cabinet. "When are you going to shut up about that?" he asked. "I'm tired of hearing it. And if you think I'm going to admit you were right, you're crazy."

Big Jed stormed past Chet and out the door. He went over to the bunkhouse, where the hands who hadn't gone to Chico had been awaiting orders to go up on Canyon Mountain. Then Big Jed and Chet led the hands through the darkness toward the corrals. They hurried to saddle their horses in the light of the barn. There was a lot to do and most of the night had slipped past.

Big Jed was cursing and raving about the circumstances continually. There was no way they were ever going to be able to get up onto the mountain and get the rustling done before daybreak.

But there was no stopping now. The helicopter was on its way and there was just this one last effort left before the Green Ranch would fall into financial ruin and he could take it over. Barlow didn't intend to let this one last opportunity slip past him, even if it meant taking a chance in the light of early morning.

Now Big Jed Barlow cared only about getting up onto Canyon Mountain with his hands and rustling that last Charolais bull and the cattle in the pasture. He could deal with whatever had happened to Foster and the others later. If he wasn't successful in what he had to do right away, nothing else would matter anyway.

Big Jed and Chet were getting ready to mount their horses when a pickup appeared in the yard. Everyone had their guns ready, but lowered them when a beaten Brice Foster hobbled into the barn.

Everyone stood speechless for a time. Finally, it was Chet who spoke up.

"Foster, you've got to be the dumbest bastard on earth. You couldn't screw up much worse."

Foster lunged at Chet. The two went down into the straw on the dirt floor, punching and kicking and raising a lot of dust. Big Jed yelled twice and they still fought. The hands all set to breaking the fight up and finally the two were pulled apart.

"You two can save that for later," Big Jed told them. "That helicopter is on its way and we've wasted way too much time already."

"Aren't you going to ask him what the hell happened at Chico?" Chet wanted to know.

"What the hell difference does it make now?" Big Jed yelled. "We've got work to do. Let's go!"

Foster saddled a horse for himself, his pain evident with every movement. From the dried blood on his face and the torn clothes, Chet concluded the fight must have been a bad one. They all watched Foster and when he had his horse saddled, Big Jed threw him a box of ampules and a vial and syringe.

"Have you forgotten how to use that?" he asked Foster.

"No," Foster said.

"Are your hands too broken up to change brands?" he asked.

Again, Foster answered no.

"Good," Big Jed said. " 'Cause if you had told me you couldn't do your job, you would be a dead man. Now, let's ride up Canyon Mountain.

Dan led the patrol in his Jeep and when they arrived at the Green Ranch, Lucy was headed for the corrals. She stopped to watch them drive in and turned for the barn. Dan got out of his Jeep and followed her.

Dan came into the barn and saw her putting a saddle on her palomino. Lucy spoke up before Dan had a chance to ask her what she was doing.

"I heard a helicopter again up on Canyon Mountain," she said. "I heard about what happened at Chico and I didn't think you could get here. So I wasn't about to wait around and let Barlow try it again."

"What did you think you could do alone?" Dan asked.

"I would have done as much as I could," she answered. "If we lose this ranch, Mother will die. I decided I wasn't going to just sit and let that happen without at least taking Big Jed Barlow down with her."

The hands were all in the barn now, selecting saddles for themselves and for the deputies who came with Dan. They went into the corral and brought a number of horses back into the barn to saddle.

"You don't need to put yourself in danger now," Dan said. "We can take care of things from here."

"Not a chance!" Lucy said. "You aren't keeping me off that mountain for any reason. You know I couldn't stand to be down here, wondering what was happening up on top."

"There's no need to risk being injured or killed," Dan said. "That isn't being very smart."

"No one ever accused me of being very smart," Lucy said.

"I wish you would just let me take it from here," Dan said. "I've deputized what's left of your hired hands."

"I see only three," Lucy said.

"That's all there are now," Dan said. He decided there was no use in prolonging the news about Ben Hutton. "I'm sorry to tell you I had to shoot Ben Hutton."

Lucy showed no real expression. Dan could see

that she had no feelings as such left for the man, but was sorry he had had to die in the manner he did.

"I guess that's how he wanted to go out, wasn't it?" Lucy finally said. "He wanted to have everybody think of him as some kind of hero. Too bad he couldn't just face reality and make something of himself. What about Brice Foster?"

"He must have slipped away somehow," Dan said. "He's likely with Big Jed Barlow now."

Lucy nodded. She got on her palomino and ignored Dan when he tried again to talk her out of going up on top. He talked to her while the others mounted up and then he got on his horse. Lucy had turned in the saddle and she was facing him.

"You might as well stop insisting that I remain down here," she said. "If you want to hog-tie me and hold me, then you'll have to leave some of your men to watch me. I don't think you want to do that."

Dan saw no point in arguing with her. He could order her not to go, but she would likely ignore him. There was no law against riding up on Canyon Mountain—even if there was going to be a gun battle with Big Jed Barlow and his Cross 12 hands.

Big Jed Barlow led his men up on top and looked out across the open meadow. It was still dark but he could see that the Green Ranch cattle were bunched together at the other end, near the water trough and corrals. He yelled for everyone to get busy, there was no time to lose.

The helicopter was sitting in the middle of the pasture, the rotor blades turning slowly. The pilot got out and came over to Big Jed.

"It's going to be light soon," he said. "What the hell kept you?"

"Problems," Big Jed told him. "But we've got it taken care of."

Big Jed left one of the hands to stay with the pilot and guard the helicopter, just in case something went wrong. That was standard procedure. It had worked well when Jack Green had showed up; the hand had gotten into the helicopter with the pilot and he could have shot Green from the helicopter if Green hadn't fallen off the cliff first.

Big Jed took his hands toward the herd, eager to get the bull off the mountain before daybreak. Dawn wasn't far away, as the eastern sky was starting to turn a dull gray along the horizon.

Brice Foster fumbled with the tranquilizer gun and the syringes that carried the drugs for putting the bull to sleep. His hands hurt him terribly and though he had told Big Jed down below that he could do his job, he wasn't so sure now.

Chet Barlow was sniping at him continuously about what had happened and how he was going to be glad when this was over. Foster was getting tired of hearing Chet tell him how things would get back to normal a lot faster once he was gone.

More than once Foster had warned Chet to keep his mouth shut. He told Chet he didn't care what he said after the job was over, but at least to wait until then to make trouble.

But Chet wasn't listening. He continued to pick on Foster and to tell him there was no reason for the things he had done while he had been working for the Cross 12. He worked to make Foster madder and madder.

Asking Big Jed to put a stop to it didn't even help. All Big Jed would say to Foster was, "Ignore it. You've got a job to do."

While Big Jed and the other hands worked to separate the bull from the rest of the herd, Foster spent time trying to get the tranquilizer gun ready. He realized that a couple of his knuckles were broken from the fighting; they were now swollen badly, making it very difficult to do the measuring and placement of the syringe into the tranquilizer gun.

Big Jed and the other hands were having trouble getting the bull to settle down. The bull wanted to stay with the rest of the herd and it was a continual chore for Big Jed and his hands to keep the bull apart from them.

"What the hell is keeping you, Foster?" Big Jed yelled over. "Get over here and put this bull to sleep. We haven't got all night up here!"

Foster had just gotten the tranquilizer gun together and was just getting into the saddle to start over when Chet showed up.

"Damnit, Foster," Chet said, "you're going to screw this up as well. Give me that gun."

"I can do it," Foster said.

Chet raised up in the saddle. "I said give me the gun!"

Foster turned the gun on Chet and said, "Let's see if it works first."

Chet sat on his horse in shocked surprise while Foster stuck the barrel of the tranquilizer gun up to his neck and pulled the trigger. The needle entered his throat and spilled its contents into his jugular vein. He grabbed his throat and gasped and jumped down off his horse, then stumbled to the ground.

In a matter of moments Chet was lying still in the grass, the needle sticking out of his throat. Big Jed and some of the other hands were looking over to see what was going on and Foster knew he had one chance now, and that was to run.

All the trouble and all the time put into getting his last job done so he could get paid was now wasted. Foster realized that he would never get the money from Big Jed Barlow now and if he didn't get clear off the mountain right away, he would never get back to Nevada.

Foster kicked his horse into a dead run across the pasture. Big Jed and the Cross 12 hands were all gathered around Chet now and as soon as they realized what had happened, they started out after Foster.

Big Jed yelled for the helicopter pilot to get into the air and head Foster off from escape. The rotor blades worked themselves into a heavy spin and the craft lifted off the ground and into the air.

Foster was headed for the Green Ranch side of Canyon Mountain. He realized that was the shortest and fastest way down. And with the helicopter after him as well, he would need a lot of luck. If he could just get a good head start, he would be gone and he wouldn't come back. But if he let Big Jed and the Cross 12 hands catch him now, there would be no tomorrow.

Chapter Twenty

Dan worried that his manpower was too low to cover all the trails coming down off Canyon Mountain. He didn't want to give Big Jed Barlow or any of his hands an avenue of escape. It would be hard enough to contain them just on top in the meadow.

As best he could, Dan divided up his deputies and sent Leon and four men around the back of the mountain to come up the trail Barlow had likely taken with his men. Other deputies were scattered out to find any and every trail that might come down off the mountain.

Dan and Lucy worked their way up the mountain toward where the trail skirted the high cliff and came out on top. It was still dark but they could both hear the sound of a helicopter on top and realized that Big Jed and his Cross 12 hands were already at work.

Dan found himself and Lucy at the base of the steep trail when a rider appeared in front of them. The rider appeared to be in a big hurry, as the helicopter was coming along the side of the cliff and up behind him.

The helicopter turned to slow down above the rider and Dan could see a man with a rifle on the passenger side pointing to him and Lucy. The helicopter then swerved away.

Dan recognized the rider as Brice Foster. Foster stopped his horse and turned around, as if to decide whether or not he wanted to try and go back up the trail. But he remained stopped on his horse and when Dan leveled his rifle on him and told him to freeze, he stayed put.

The helicopter roared over once again as Dan made Foster get down off his horse. Dan then handcuffed Foster to a tree and told him his best bet was to stay there and wait for everything to get over. Foster said nothing, but sat down to wait.

Dan got back on his horse and he and Lucy continued up the steep trail along the cliff, while the helicopter came down from the sky toward the mountain once again.

The helicopter had a bright searchlight which came on and locked in on Dan and Lucy as they tried to maneuver their horses along the trail. The light and the noise began to frighten the horses badly.

"Hold on," Dan said. "We have to get past this cliff or we're going to be in trouble."

"We're already in trouble," Lucy said.

She worked her palomino as best she could along the trail above the cliff, while the helicopter roared past them just overhead, the light streaming down onto them. Dan was having trouble with his horse as well and held the reins tight to avoid letting the stallion break into a run. The footing was too treacherous and they would go over the cliff.

The helicopter turned and held position in the air as the gunman on the passenger side opened fire. Dan and Lucy both heard bullets whining off the rocks all around them. Finally, the gunman had to reload.

The helicopter turned out for another run at them and Dan realized the gunman might not miss this time. There was no choice but to let the horses go into a run. They were taking a grave chance with footing. But if they didn't get across, the gunman would either get them or the helicopter would force them over the cliff.

Dan held his stallion to the trail and Lucy did the same. There was a clump of trees at the edge of the cliff and they made for it, urging the horses faster once they cleared the steep trail.

Dan and Lucy reached the trees just as the helicopter swooped over again. This time Dan felt a bullet just graze his left shoulder. But he and Lucy managed to get into the trees and settle their horses down.

Daylight was breaking over the mountain and in the pasture, Dan could see riders coming toward them. Big Jed Barlow was leading them. They seemed to be coming as if they had been chasing somebody, for when they saw Dan and Lucy they held up for a moment.

Dan realized he could not stand off the helicopter and the Cross 12 hands at the same time.

"If you really know how to use that rifle," Dan said to Lucy, "now's the time to show me."

Big Jed Barlow decided he was going to take his hands after Dan and Lucy, and came ahead again. Dan and Lucy both began to fire at the Cross 12 cowhands as they came charging across the meadow at them. Two men fell and the others turned off. Lucy reloaded her rifle while Dan got ready for the helicopter as it made another pass toward them.

The helicopter came toward them, shining the bright spotlight down into the timber once again. Dan waited until the helicopter slowed to make a turn sideways. This would allow the gunman in the helicopter to open fire again. But it also allowed Dan a clear shot at both the gunman and the spotlight.

Dan fired up into the helicopter repeatedly. His bullets brought the gunman screaming down out of the helicopter. He fell headlong through the dawn light into the trees way downslope. Dan also managed to shoot the spotlight out and it went with a loud pop and a shower of fine glass.

Lucy began firing now as well. She was working to keep the Cross 12 hands from overrunning them in the trees. She fired at moving men in the early morning shadows while Dan continued to pump bullets up into the helicopter.

After firing until his rifle was empty, Dan could see that he had done considerable damage to the helicopter's fuel system. The engine began to sputter and an acrid cloud of black smoke poured out of the helicopter as it turned and swung away through the dawn sky.

The smoke that trailed from the helicopter became thicker and thicker, sending a heavy streamer of black out into the clear sky. Dan and Lucy watched as the helicopter began to swerve downward in a semi-circle toward the ground.

The pilot tried to steer the craft back up but succeeded only in getting the direction of his fate changed. Within seconds the craft arched over onto its back in midair and smashed into the side of the rock cliff, exploding into a huge ball of orange and black.

The sound was a tremendous blast and Dan knew it caused fear among the Cross 12 hands. Their mightiest weapon was now a heap of tangled metal at the bottom of the cliff.

Now Dan turned his attention again to Big Jed Barlow and the Cross 12 hands. They were panicking, as Leon and the other deputies were raiding up on them from behind. The helicopter crash had also demoralized them to a degree and all of Big Jed Barlow's yelling could not keep them together.

Dan took the opportunity to move against them and began to fire his rifle into them as they retreated back toward the other end of the meadow. Lucy was right behind Dan, kicking her palomino into a run to catch up to the sorrel stallion.

Big Jed Barlow broke off from the main group and ran his horse out of the meadow and into the trees along the slope of the mountain. Leon and the rest of the deputies were surrounding the Cross 12 hands and they were giving up. Dan knew his last effort had to be to stop Big Jed.

"I'm going after him," Dan told Lucy. "Stay here where you can help Leon and show him where Foster is."

"Be careful, Dan," Lucy said. "Barlow knows that country on the other side of the mountain. He could lead you into an ambush."

Dan took the sorrel stallion and raced across the meadow to where Barlow had gone into the trees. The trail ahead was treacherous and lined with trees and rocks—an excellent spot for an ambush.

Dan took his time, realizing that to make himself go too fast could be fatal.

After a period of time, Dan realized he was being led in a long, twisted trail that went down the back side of the mountain toward the Cross 12 Ranch. He continued to work his way along but realized almost too late that Barlow knew the country well and was setting him up.

It was Lucy's yell that made him duck down off his horse just as a bullet whizzed overhead from the rocks above the trail. Barlow had worked himself around and had come up above Dan along the trail.

"Dan, he's above you!" Lucy was yelling. "I can

see him up here!"

Lucy knew the country on the back side of the mountain and she had ridden behind Dan, just to see where Barlow was going to take him. Now Dan could hear gunfire up above him where Lucy was, a gun battle between Lucy and Big Jed Barlow.

Dan worked his way up along the side of the hill as the firing continued. He found his way to Lucy, who had Barlow pinned down behind some rocks.

"I have to thank you," Dan told Lucy. "You saved my life."

"I told you he was going to do this," Lucy said.

Dan could see where Barlow was hiding and yelled out to him.

"It's time to give up, Barlow! You can't get out of this now."

Big Jed Barlow answered by firing repeatedly at Dan and Lucy's position. He shot until he had emptied his rifle, and then yelled back at Dan.

"You ain't taking me! You had just as well get that through your head, Slayter."

"We've got you trapped," Dan told him. "You can't possibly get away."

Barlow had by now reloaded his rifle and again opened fire. Dan and Lucy stayed under cover until he was again empty.

"I'm going to move around to the side," Dan said. "You stay here under cover. I'm going to get him out of there one way or another."

As Big Jed Barlow loaded his rifle, Dan crept through the rocks and timber. He moved cautiously to where he had a position looking down at Barlow. He worked his way down slowly as Barlow looked out in the direction of where he had been resting under cover with Lucy.

Dan took position behind a tree and pulled his revolver.

"It's over, Barlow. Give up now."

Barlow turned in surprise and began shooting wildly. The bullets pummeled the tree where Dan had taken position and Dan reached around to fire at Barlow.

Barlow was a madman, coming out of his hiding position up the hill toward Dan, levering bullets into his rifle and firing as he went. Dan's first bullet caught him square in the chest and the big man stopped and gasped.

"No more shooting!" Dan ordered.

But Big Jed Barlow wasn't going to give up and he wasn't going to be stopped by just one bullet. He pushed cartridges into his rifle and cursed at Dan while his eyes glazed. He levered the rifle and got ready to shoot again.

Dan opened up with his pistol, fanning four bullets into the middle of the big man. Big Jed Barlow had by now taken five bullets and he still wasn't down.

Barlow continued to shoot, but his aim was wild and the bullets went everywhere. Dan stood behind the tree reloading as the huge man came up the slope, his front a mass of blood. It seemed impossible he could still be on his feet.

Dan's next shots were meant for the head and neck region. Again he fanned bullets into Barlow, this time making two neat holes in the big man's forehead. Big Jed Barlow dropped heavily to the ground and kicked for a time until he finally lay still.

Lucy came up behind Dan and turned away from the sight.

"That man wasn't going to ever stop what he wanted to do to the Green Ranch," she said. "His intentions were to get what he wanted, or die trying."

"It appears that way," Dan said. "I've never seen a man so obsessed with something. But it's over now and the Green Ranch can prosper."

Dan and Lucy went back to where Leon and the other deputies were preparing the Cross 12 cowhands for the long ride down the mountain to jail. Dan knew there would be a long investigation into what all had gone on at the Cross 12 and what had caused everything to happen the way it did.

Brice Foster could be the key to some of those answers. Dan found him resting comfortably where he had handcuffed him to the tree. Leon took him and they started down the mountain.

Lucy made sure there was enough water in the troughs for the herd and watched the big Charolais bull graze for a while before she started back with Dan.

"Do you think you'll ever leave law enforcement and settle down?" she asked Dan.

"I don't know, but not for a while," Dan answered. "I wish you and your mother luck with the ranch. Maybe you can even take over the Cross Twelve Ranch now. However it runs out, I know you'll do well."

The sun was now full above the eastern horizon and the day was open and clear. Dan and Lucy made their way across the trail along the cliff and Dan took one last look across the open meadow and saw for the first time in over a hundred years that there was peace on Canyon Mountain.

POWELL'S ARMY
BY TERENCE DUNCAN

#1: UNCHAINED LIGHTNING   (1994, $2.50)

Thundering out of the past, a trio of deadly enforcers dispenses its own brand of frontier justice throughout the untamed American West! Two men and one woman, they are the U.S. Army's most lethal secret weapon—they are POWELL'S ARMY!

#2: APACHE RAIDERS   (2073, $2.50)

The disappearance of seventeen Apache maidens brings tribal unrest to the violent breaking point. To prevent an explosion of bloodshed, Powell's Army races through a nightmare world south of the border—and into the deadly clutches of a vicious band of Mexican flesh merchants!

#3: MUSTANG WARRIORS   (2171, $2.50)

Someone is selling cavalry guns and horses to the Comanche—and that spells trouble for the bluecoats' campaign against Chief Quanah Parker's bloodthirsty Kwahadi warriors. But Powell's Army are no strangers to trouble. When the showdown comes, they'll be ready—and someone is going to die!

#4: ROBBERS ROOST   (2285, $2.50)

After hijacking an army payroll wagon and killing the troopers riding guard, Three-Fingered Jack and his gang high-tail it into Virginia City to spend their ill-gotten gains. But Powell's Army plans to apprehend the murderous hardcases before the local vigilantes do—to make sure that Jack and his slimy band stretch hemp the legal way!

Available wherever paperbacks are sold, or order direct from the Publisher. Send cover price plus 50¢ per copy for mailing and handling to Zebra Books, Dept. 2413, 475 Park Avenue South, New York, N.Y. 10016. Residents of New York, New Jersey and Pennsylvania must include sales tax. DO NOT SEND CASH.